Minor Detail

MINOR DETAIL

Adania Shibli

translated by Elisabeth Jaquette

A NEW DIRECTIONS BOOK

Originally published in English translation by Fitzcarraldo Editions in Great Britain in 2020

Manufactured in the United States of America
First published as a New Directions Paperbook (ndp1482) in 2020
New Directions Books are printed on acid-free paper

Library of Congress Cataloging-in-Publication Data
Names: Shiblī, ʿAdanīyah, author. | Jaquette, Elisabeth, translator.
Title: Minor detail / Adania Shibli ; translated by Elisabeth Jaquette.
Other titles: Tafāṣīl thānawī. English
Description: New York : New Directions Publishing Corporation, 2020. |
First published in Arabic by Dar Al Adab: Beirut, Lebanon. |
Translated from the Arabic.
Identifiers: LCCN 2020004677 | ISBN 9780811229074 (paperback ; acid-free paper) |
ISBN 9780811229081 (ebook)
Subjects: LCSH: Arab-Israeli conflict—1948–1967—Fiction.
Classification: LCC PJ7962.H425 T3413 2020 | DDC 892.7/37—dc23
LC record available at https://lccn.loc.gov/2020004677

2 4 6 8 10 9 7 5 3 1

New Directions Books are published for James Laughlin
by New Directions Publishing Corporation
80 Eighth Avenue, New York 10011

Minor Detail

— 1 —

Nothing moved except the mirage. Vast stretches of barren hills rose in layers up to the sky, trembling silently under the heft of the mirage, while the harsh afternoon sunlight blurred the outlines of the pale yellow ridges. The only details that could be discerned were a faint winding border which aimlessly meandered across these ridges, and the slender shadows of dry, thorny burnet and stones dotting the ground. Aside from these, nothing at all, just a great expanse of the arid Negev desert, over which crouched the intense August heat.

The only signs of life in the area were distant barking and the noise of soldiers working to set up camp. These reached his ears as he gazed through binoculars from his position atop a hill, examining the scene before him. Against the sun's harsh glare, he carefully followed the course of narrow paths across the sand, occasionally pausing to fix his gaze on a ridge for a moment longer. Finally, he lowered his binoculars, wiped off the sweat, and returned them to their case. Then he began making his way through the thick, heavy afternoon air, back to the camp.

When they had arrived, they found two standing huts and the remains of a wall in a partially destroyed third. It was all that had survived in this place after the heavy shelling the area had experienced at the beginning of the war. But now a command tent and mess tent were pitched next to these huts, and the sounds of hammering stakes and clattering poles filled the air as the soldiers worked to pitch the three tents that would serve as their quarters. His deputy, the sergeant major, met him upon his return, and informed him that the men had removed all the rubble and stones from the area, and that a group of soldiers was working to rebuild the trenches. He replied that all preparations must be finished before nightfall, then told him to order the division sergeants and some corporals and experienced soldiers to report for a meeting in the command tent immediately.

* * *

Afternoon sunlight filled the entrance to the tent, streamed through it and spread across the sand, revealing little indentations on its surface made by the soldiers' feet. He began the briefing by explaining that their primary mission during their presence here, in addition to demarcating the southern border with Egypt and preventing anyone from penetrating it, was to comb the southwest part of the Negev and cleanse it of any remaining Arabs. Air Force sources had reported movements here, of Arabs and infiltrators in the area. They would also undertake daily reconnaissance patrols, to explore and familiarize themselves with the region. This operation could take some time, but they were to remain stationed here until security in this part of the Negev had been established. They would also run daily drills and military maneuvers with the soldiers, to train them in desert combat and acclimatize them to the conditions.

The soldiers in attendance listened as they followed the movement of his hands over the map laid out in front of them, where the camp's position appeared in the form of a small, barely discernible black dot inside a large gray triangle. None of them commented on what was said, and silence filled the tent for several seconds. The officer turned his gaze from the map to their sullen faces, dripping with sweat, glistening in the light that came through the entrance to the tent. After a pause he continued, instructing them to be sure that the soldiers, especially those who had recently joined the platoon, took good care of their uniforms and gear; if anyone lacked clothing or equipment, they should notify him immediately. The soldiers should also be reminded of the importance of maintaining personal hygiene, and shaving daily. Then, before adjourning the meeting, he turned to the driver, a sergeant, and two corporals who were present, and ordered them to prepare to depart with him on a preliminary reconnaissance patrol of the area.

Before the patrol, he stopped by one of the huts, which he had taken as his quarters, and began moving his belongings from the entrance, where he had stacked them, to a corner of the room. Then he took a jerry can from the stack, and poured water from it into a small tin bowl. He took a towel from his kit bag, dipped it in the water he had poured into the bowl, and used it to wipe the sweat from his face. He rinsed the towel, then took off his shirt and wiped his armpits. He put his shirt back on, buttoned it up, then rinsed the towel thoroughly and hung it on one of the old nails that remained in the wall. Then he took the bowl outside, poured the dirty water onto the sand, went back into the room, put the bowl in the corner with the rest of his belongings and left.

The driver was sitting in his seat behind the steering wheel, while the rest of the group that had been ordered to join him were standing around the vehicle. As he approached, they climbed in the back, and he took the front passenger seat. The driver adjusted his position before reaching for the ignition switch and starting the engine, which released a loud roar out into the open space.

They set off west, forging their way through pale yellow hills that extended in every direction. Thick clouds of sand sprung from underneath the vehicle's tires, rose up and followed after them, completely obscuring the view behind. Some sand struck those seated in the back, forcing them to shut their eyes and mouths in an attempt to keep the dust out. The waves of sand, with their shifting shapes, would not settle until the vehicle had vanished far into the distance and the sound of its engine had entirely faded. Only then did the sand drift gradually back onto the hills, softening the sharp parallel tracks left by the vehicle's tires.

They reached the armistice line with Egypt and examined the border, but observed no attempts to breach it. By the time the sun neared the line of the horizon, the dust and heat had conquered them, and he ordered the driver to return to camp. They had not encountered any life on their patrol of the area, despite the reports indicating movement there.

Though they arrived back at camp before nightfall, to the east the blue sky had nearly given way to darkness and the faint glow of a few stars had already appeared. Preparations in the camp had not yet been finished, and after stepping down from the vehicle he announced that everything must be completed before they sat down to dinner. That enlivened the soldiers, and their silhouettes began moving more quickly and animatedly around the camp.

He headed into his hut, where darkness had taken hold, so he paused for a moment, then went back to the door and opened it wide, to ease the darkness inside. He took the towel, now completely dry, from where it hung on the wall. He dampened it by pouring water directly onto it from the jerry can, then wiped the sweat and dust from his face and hands. He bent over his belongings again, picked up a lantern, lifted the glass, then placed it on the table without lighting the mantle, and left the hut.

Even though he had been inside for only a few minutes, the sky was now speckled with stars, and darkness had enveloped the hills so completely that night seemed to have descended upon the camp all at once. The soldiers' silhouettes were moving slowly again, and their voices pierced the deep blue night, while the glow of lanterns sneaked through the cracks and openings of the tents.

He set off on a tour of the camp facilities, and inspected the progress of the work throughout, especially the process of rebuilding trenches and readying the drill areas. Things seemed to be going according to plan, except that it was past eight p.m., and usually they gathered to eat at eight sharp. Before long, they all headed to the mess tent to sit down around the dinner tables.

After dinner he walked to his hut, guided by the light of the full moon and the stars scattered above the dark line of the horizon. He prepared himself for bed, then extinguished the lantern and lay down. He pushed the sheets far away, leaving his body completely exposed; the heat weighing on the room was intense, but despite it he fell straight asleep. It had been a long, hard day for everyone: August 9, 1949.

* * *

He was awakened by movement on his left thigh. He opened his eyes to the utter darkness and extreme heat in the room. His body was dripping with sweat. There was a creature just below the hem of his underpants; it moved higher, then stopped. The hum of emptiness continued to fill the space, occasionally punctuated by the muffled sounds of the soldiers assigned to guard the camp, the wind slapping at tent roofs, the distant howling of a dog, maybe the groaning of camels.

After a moment of stillness, he sat up in one gentle motion. At this the creature moved again, so he held still, then shifted his gaze toward his leg. The darkness concealed whatever was on him, though it was now possible to distinguish the silhouettes of the furniture, his belongings, and the wooden beams on which the roof panels rested. Through cracks in the ceiling, a dim light filtered down into the hut from the moon outside. Suddenly his hand lunged at the creature and flung it off his thigh, then he leapt to the lantern on the table and lit it. As soon as the mantle glowed with flame, he circled the lantern over the area between the table and bed. There was no movement, except for the swaying shadows of a few scattered pebbles on the floor, as the lantern hovered over the area. He expanded his orbit to include the bed, then under it, then each corner of the room, and the area by the door, then around his bag and trunk, and the rest of his belongings, then the walls, up toward the ceiling, and the bed again, and around his boots; then he shook his clothes that were hanging on the nails in the wall, looked under the bed once more, and across the entire floor, patiently, including all the corners, then back to the walls and the ceiling, and finally his shadow, which was leaping around him, swinging aimlessly from one side to the other. Then he calmed down, and the light calmed with him, as did the shadows in the room. He brought the lantern close to his thigh, where a slight burning sensation was starting to spread. Under the light, two small red dots appeared. It seemed the creature had been faster than he was, and bit him before he had cast it away.

He extinguished the lantern, set it beside the trunk, and returned to bed, though he did not manage to fall back asleep.

The burning sensation from the bite on his thigh gradually intensified, and by dawn it felt as if he were being flayed alive.

Eventually he got out of bed and went to the corner where his belongings were stacked, now dappled in the morning sunlight seeping down through holes in the ceiling. He filled the tin bowl with water, took the towel from the nail where it was hanging, dipped it in the bowl before wringing it out, then wiped down his face, chest, back, and armpits. He put on his shirt, then his pants, pulling them up just past the knees before pausing to examine the bite on his thigh. A slight swelling had now formed around the two dots, which had turned black and were pulsating with pain. He pulled his pants up all the way, tucked in his shirt, then tightened his belt around his waist, buckling it at the visible crease in the fabric. He rinsed the towel, returned it to its place on the nail, cast an unhurried look at the walls, ceiling, and floor, and left.

* * *

They concluded that morning's reconnaissance patrol as the sun was still approaching the center of the sky. They could no longer bear the scorching heat, nor sitting in the vehicle, where the metal was so hot in places that it lashed at anyone who touched it. Before noon, August 10, 1949.

The soldiers in the camp sought refuge in the narrow strips of shade alongside the tents, and avoided the ground that lay directly in the sun, where every grain of sand absorbed heat from the rays that had shone on them since morning. As for him, it was not the scorching heat but a sharp stomach pain that struck during the patrol, and forced him to his hut as soon as he stepped down from the vehicle, without stopping at the command tent or inspecting the camp.

The dirty water from his wash that morning was still idling

in the tin bowl. He carried it outside and emptied it onto the sand near the hut. Then he filled it again with clean water from the jerry can. He undressed down to his underpants, took the towel hanging from the nail, dipped it in the bowl and began to wipe down his body. He began with his face, then moved to his neck, his chest, and as much of his back as he could reach. He rinsed the towel, then wiped down his arms and armpits. His legs were the last thing he cleaned, avoiding the area around the bite, which had grown redder and more swollen. After he rinsed the towel well and hung it on the nail, he picked up a small box that was sitting in the corner with his belongings and carried it to the table. He set it down, opened the lid and took out antiseptic, cotton, and gauze. He put some antiseptic on the cotton and began cleaning the area around the bite very carefully. When he finished, he wrapped his thigh with the gauze, headed to bed and lay down. Intense cramps had begun gripping his back and shoulders.

* * *

Although the afternoon patrol was useful for exploring the area's more hidden spots, no infiltrators were found on that patrol either. The repetitive sand dunes encircling them from every direction remained silent, and revealed no tracks aside from the vehicle's own.

Meanwhile, at the camp, as the day proceeded and the heat raged, the soldiers continued their slow march trailing the shade, following as it moved across stretches of sand alongside the tents. When he returned from the patrol, he headed to a group that included a few experienced soldiers, even though his stomachache had grown worse. He briefed them on the details of the day's two patrols, before inquiring how they were acclimatizing to the conditions and heat, especially during their drills. After listening to their clipped replies, he emphasized the importance of them being here, and of the drills, which were no less critical than participating in missions outside the camp. It was their presence and perseverance, regardless of which military operations they took part in, which were crucial to securing control over the area, enforcing the new border with Egypt and preventing infiltrators from penetrating it. They were the first and only platoon to arrive this far south since the armistice had been declared, and they had been given complete responsibility for maintaining security in the area.

On the way to his hut he passed the command tent, where his deputy, the division sergeants and the driver were resting after their afternoon patrol, and he informed them they would be conducting another patrol before sunset.

* * *

Then another patrol, and another the next day, and the day after that, yet all the area revealed were sandstorms and dust clouds, which seemed intent on chasing and harrying them. But these storms did not succeed in stopping their patrols, nor did the stillness of the barren hills weaken his resolve to find any remaining Arabs in the area and capture the infiltrators among them, who rushed to hide behind the dunes when they heard the vehicle's roar. Their slender black shadows sometimes wavered in front of him, trembling between the hills, but whenever the vehicle raced toward them, they found no one when they arrived.

Only the intense heat or darkness could put an end to these pursuits; only when they could no longer bear the blazing sun, or when night began to fall, would he tell the driver to return them to camp.

And with nightfall the air grew less heavy and dense, while

retaining a tolerable degree of heat. This enlivened the soldiers, most of whom, since their arrival, had not left the camp, or even the strips of shade by the tents, where they sought refuge each day when they finished their drills. And so, in the evening, the sound of their conversations and laughter rumbled through the area, until ten p.m., when they retired to their tents and he went to his hut.

Inside, the darkness was thick and strong. From time to time noises would seep into the space, at first sounding like murmurs and snippets of unintelligible clamor, until it gradually became possible to distinguish the sound of wind slapping the tent roofs, the footfalls of soldiers patrolling the camp and their abrupt calls, all of which were interspersed with distant sounds of gunshots, dogs barking, and maybe camels groaning.

* * *

He was sweating, straining to breathe the room's heavy air, as he sat at the table with several maps spread in front of him. The distant sounds reached him from outside, deepening the ache in his head. He had not undressed or even removed his boots now filled with sweat and drenching his toes, which had been confined in them since the morning. It was approaching midnight: August 11, 1949. He slowly drew his hand to the edge of the table, bent his knees and began to stand up, but he staggered and quickly gripped the chair, supporting his body with both hands. He took a deep breath. On his second attempt he managed to stand, then walked over to the trunk in the corner of the room, bent over it, placed his hands on the locks, opened them, and lifted the lid. He reached inside with his right hand and took out some box magazines. He stood up again, went back to the table, set down the magazines, and then, with trembling hands, began carefully placing them in his pouch, as sweat dripped from his hairline down his temples and cheeks. When he had finished, he picked up his gun from where it was leaning against the table, slung it over his shoulder, and left the hut.

The darkness outside seemed less intense, although the full moon was now two nights past. He paused for a moment at the entrance gate, waiting for the soldiers on guard to open it, then set off west, toward the jet-black hills which gently swallowed him whole.

* * *

He walked for a long time, gripped by the sharp stomachache and cramps in his back. The sand stretched beneath his feet in dips and rises that periodically caught him off-balance, making him stumble and nearly trip. Despite this he pressed on into the darkness, while every so often, from between the folds of night, distant wailing sounds floated up, until a steep decline took him by surprise and tossed him to the bottom of the slope.

When the sand finally stopped dragging him down, he tried to stand, but severe cramps in his feet and hands dropped him back to the ground. He shifted the position of his body slightly, so that he was more or less seated, then inhaled deeply. This calmed his shaky breathing, but did not ease the tightness in his chest.

He remained still, his eyes fixed on the expanses extending before him and sated by the darkness. His left hand rested on his thigh, feeling the bite through the fabric of his pants. His heart had been beating so hard while he was falling that it had felt like he was choking, but after several minutes it slowed to its usual pace. He turned his head to the right, then to the left. He was alone among the hills. He lifted his gaze to the stars scattered across the sky, then to the peaks of the hills, and to the moon carving a path between them, toward the dark line of the western horizon.

He lifted his hand from his leg, placed it beside him on the sand and pressed himself up. Immediately, he lost his balance and almost fell, but he caught himself and managed to stay upright. He headed directly for the hill that rose before him, and when he reached it he began to climb, letting darkness fill his eyes until he reached the top. And there at the summit he stood for some time, gazing out into the darkness enveloping him. Intermittent wailing sounds brushed his ears, hesitantly, and the hills echoed the sound, making it impossible to determine which direction it was coming from. They seemed to be part of the darkness that crouched on the sandy expanses unfolding in every direction. Then he continued walking.

* * *

He kept walking until the end of night, when the darkness began to dissolve and the folds of the hills were revealed under the light of dawn. By then the air still held a slight chill, which penetrated his clothes and crept into his body, stinging his bones. He was seized by a sudden tremor that made his body shake violently and his breathing become heavy again, forcing him to stop walking. He tried to draw a slow breath, but his throat abruptly released a cough and a belch, jerking his head down, and he began vomiting.

When the bout of nausea ended, he gripped the water bottle hanging from his waist with trembling hands, removed the cap, brought it to his lips and rinsed his mouth several times. He spat, and calmed down slightly, as the sounds coming from behind the hills returned, now louder than before. It was as if the dawn light had suddenly eliminated the distance between them. His breath became strained again, his body trembled and he quickly moved his gaze across the desolate hills besieging him from all sides. Then he set off directly toward the sounds, which were growing louder and louder, as were his heartbeats as he got closer, until it was finally possible to distinguish some of these sounds. At that point he stopped walking for a few moments. Then, despite the shivering that had overtaken him, he started up again, marching toward the sounds, which, in the end, turned out to be nothing more than the soldiers in his platoon. Fifteen minutes was all it took to return to the camp which he had left several hours before.

* * *

The faint light of early morning shrouded the hilltops surrounding the camp. The soldiers had just awoken and were milling around; some were emerging from tents or disappearing inside them, while others took a place in the queue by the water tank, towels draped over their shoulders or around their necks, waiting for their turn to use the tap. When he walked through the main gate, and past them toward his hut, each soldier straightened up and deftly raised his right hand to his head, eyes fixed forward, to salute him.

A warm darkness lurked inside the hut. He closed the door behind him and approached the table, removed his magazine pouch and set it down, then went over to the bed, leaned his gun against the wall to its right and sat down. He stayed there for a while, immobile, as the darkness receded and the room's contours gradually became clear. The cramps had settled into every part of his body. He slowly bent down to his feet and began removing his boots, which the dusty sand had turned from brown to pale yellow. He picked up the boots with both hands and rose with an effort that made him wince, then went to the door, opened it, stood just outside the hut's entrance and began beating the boots together, gradually creating a halo of dust. After that, he went back inside, pushed his boots under the chair, took off his shirt and pants and put them over the back of the chair, then walked over to the bed, sat down on the edge and stared at the bandage covering the bite on his left thigh. The yellow ointment had seeped through to the surface of the white gauze. He lifted his head and let his eyes wander around the room, avoiding the morning light where it pierced through the cracks. When he finished inspecting the room, he eased himself onto the bed and lay down. Immediately black dots began dancing before his eyes, followed by the objects in the room, starting with the table, then the magazine pouch, then the trunk, the bowl, the nails in the wall, his clothes on the chair, then his boots underneath it; patches of light splintered across the roof panels and the door, then the camp, the dark dunes, the slope he fell down and the sand he tried to hold onto, then the moon, the dim horizon, his clothes on the chair, the nails in the wall, and the bandage as he unwound it from his leg. Then he leapt up from the bed. He sat back down. The bandage was still in place. After a long moment, he brought his hand to the bandage and began to unravel it. With every half wrap, one hand took the strip of gauze from the other hand, and each time the ointment's yellow hue reappeared in a certain spot, each time the color was stronger than the last, until he had undone the whole strip of gauze. And when he turned his gaze to the bite itself, he leapt from the bed, head up, and swallowed quickly several times. He looked at the strip of gauze dangling from his right hand. Aside from traces of ointment dotting its length, several sections of the fabric were disfigured. He crossed the room to the table, set the gauze down next to the magazine pouch, then lowered his head and examined the swelling on his thigh. It was filled with pus in the center, and ringed with a red circle, then a blue circle, then black.

He used half of the water left in the jerry can to wash his body, then selected a clean set of clothes from his bag, and took out a new roll of gauze, cotton, antiseptic, and a bottle of ointment from the trunk. He poured antiseptic onto the cotton and cleaned the swollen area carefully, then dipped his index finger into the ointment and rubbed it over the bite. He repeated the procedure a second time, then a third, and a fourth, until the ointment nearly concealed the swelling. After bandaging the area with the new roll of gauze, he put on clean clothes and his boots, then sat down on the edge of the bed and surrendered his ears to the sounds coming from outside, joining him in the feeble darkness that spread to every corner of the room.

Outside, the camp filled with the clamor of the soldiers' energetic movements, an occurrence that normally took place twice a day, at daybreak and nightfall, when cooler temperatures allowed them to engage in drills and to move around camp. Suddenly, he leapt from his position on the bed, crossed to a corner of the room and opened his eyes as far as his swollen eyelids allowed. He stood staring at the spot where the wall met the ceiling. A short while later, he walked to the door and opened it as wide as it would go; sharp daylight fell onto the threshold, but advanced no further to illuminate the hut's dark interior, while the voices of soldiers coming from the direction of the tents grew louder. He went back to the corner he had been inspecting and stood under it, bringing his face as close as possible, and scrutinized it again. But he did not continue this for long. After a few moments he bowed his head and began rubbing his neck, blinking intensely. He went back to the corner of the room nearest to the door and bent down. He crouched there, inspecting a particular area for a while, then turned his gaze to the corner where his belongings were stacked, and crawled toward it. When he reached the trunk, he dragged it toward him and looked behind. A slender-legged spider was clinging to the other side. He reached out with his right hand and crushed it, then crawled on toward the bed. A few small spiders nestled underneath it, and, next to them, a dead gray beetle, suspended in a web spun with their fine threads, all of which he smashed with his boots as he swept them out. He bent down again and brought his head close to the floor, inspecting it slowly. Then, without warning, he jumped around different parts of the room, crushing several small insects that were crawling on the floor.

He continued his patrol of the room, now unhurriedly combing the walls with his eyes. Two spiders and a moth; he eradicated them, then climbed onto the table, raised his head toward the ceiling and fixed his gaze on the previous corner when dark dots and lines began careening before his eyes, followed by absolute blackness. He lost his balance and nearly fell, so he quickly jumped down, pulled out a chair and collapsed into it. Then he rested his head on the edge of the table and squeezed his reddening eyelids shut.

Meanwhile, a little insect advanced toward the edge of the room and slipped through a crack between the floor and the wall, escaping into the gap.

After a while, he opened his eyes and began to blink, then lifted his head, brought his palms to his face and pressed them to his temples, his expression grim. At that moment, sounds of camels groaning and dogs barking infiltrated the space, but the sound of soldiers training and moving around the camp soon prevailed over them. He shut his eyes again. And he remained seated, surrounded by various sounds, each a different volume, tone and distance away, on that early morning, August 12, 1949.

* * *

Before long, he was climbing into the vehicle along with two sergeants and three soldiers. His gaze followed his right foot as it ascended the vehicle's step, lifted into the air and came to rest on the floor beneath the front seat, where he sank his body. To his left was the gear shift and the five dials whose hands trembled nervously, and then the black dots returned, veiling his vision for several seconds before fading, then returning again for longer.

They departed this time without opening the maps they usually studied before setting off on a patrol. Instead, he instructed the driver to head toward a certain location. "To that hill," he said curtly, aiming his hand at a ridge which was inscribed into the line of the horizon.

The vehicle's wheels devoured the sand beneath them and sprayed it ferociously into the air, transforming it into long clouds of dust that lingered behind the vehicle as usual, as they gazed at the hills that rose tirelessly on both sides of the path. Yet no sooner had they arrived at the hill he had led them to than he pointed at another, which lay on the horizon directly ahead. And so in this way they continued their patrol, moving between the hilltops, until they paused at one to inspect some tracks on the sand.

Once the engine's roar had fallen quiet and they had stepped down from the vehicle, an almost absolute calm settled upon the place, aside from the muffled sounds made by their steps on the sand as they carried out their search. When they had finished, they drank some water, returned to the vehicle and prepared to set off again, to "that hill" at which he aimed his hand from the passenger seat, before drawing a breath so deep it forced him to close his eyes. And when he opened them again, the hill he had pointed toward was obscured by black dots that leaped before his eyes like mad insects, and he raised his arm sharply, palm outstretched, making the soldiers fall silent immediately. After a moment he gestured to the driver to start the engine, but before he did, the sound of a dog barking floated up through the air.

* * *

Thorn acacia and terebinth trees appeared in the distance, preceded by cane grass, where a shallow spring skulked between the slender stalks. As soon as the vehicle stopped, he hopped from his seat and began running in the direction of the trees, taking a sandy slope that gently propelled him down, while the rest of the group followed after him. But he did not look back at them; his gaze was fixed only on the clump of trees ahead, where the sounds of a dog howling and camels groaning rose from behind their branches. When his feet landed at the base of the slope, he headed toward the vegetation, penetrating the branches, which quickly yielded to reveal a band of Arabs standing motionless by the spring. His eyes met their wide eyes, and the eyes of the startled camels, which hopped up and trotted a few steps away the moment the dog let out a howl. Then came the sound of heavy gunfire.

* * *

The dog's howling finally stopped, and a degree of calm settled over the place. Now the only sound was the muffled weeping of a girl who had curled up inside her black clothes like a beetle, and the rustle of thorn acacia, terebinth leaves, and cane grass as the soldiers moved through the spot of green surrounded by endless, barren sand dunes, combing the area for weapons, while he stood there and inspected some manure. Then he walked around the camels lying on the ground, which resembled small hills covered in dry grass. There were six of them. And although they were dead, and the sand was languidly sucking their blood into its depths, a few of their limbs still gave off slight movements. His gaze rested on a clutch of dry grass lying by the mouth of one camel; it had been ripped up by the roots, which still held suspended grains of sand.

They found no weapons. The two sergeants and soldiers combed the area several times, to no avail. Eventually he turned to the still-moaning black mass and lunged at her, grabbing her with both hands and shaking her vigorously. The dog barked louder, and she wailed louder, and the sounds merged as he pushed the girl's head into the ground, clamping his right hand over her mouth, and her sticky saliva, mucus, and tears stuck to his hand. Her smell invaded his nose, forcing him to avert his head. But a moment later he turned back toward her, then brought his other hand to his mouth, raising his index finger to his lips, and stared directly into her eyes.

* * *

When they returned to the camp, most of the soldiers were sitting in the narrow strips of shade alongside the tents, and when the girl and dog were taken down from the back of the vehicle, some soldiers left the shade and approached. He shifted his gaze from the tents to the sand, whose surface reflected the dazzling prenoon sun, then to the vehicle, which shone varying degrees of light into his eyes, prompting again the sight of black and gray dots, intensified by the flies hovering around them. At last his gaze settled on his deputy, who was asking him what they should do with the girl. For a few moments he said nothing. His jaws were stuck together so he lowered his head, closed his eyes, and took a few shallow breaths. He replied that they should put her in the other hut for the time being and assign a soldier to guard her. They would decide what to do with her later. In any case, they could not set her free in this desolate place. When he raised his head again, he looked at the soldiers who were now gathered around them and said in a clear, threatening voice not to go near the girl. Then he left them and headed for his hut.

As soon as he stepped inside, he went to the bed and lay down, closed his swollen eyelids, and was overtaken by a deep slumber.

* * *

He opened his eyes, slowly and carefully moved from his position, and sat on the edge of the bed. After a moment, he raised his left hand to his face and wiped his cheeks with his palm, then stood up, walked to the door, and opened it wide. Light entered the dim space of the hut, sneaking around his body when he peered from the doorway to inspect the area. He had not slept for long, at least not enough for the shadows to recede and expose more sand. He turned and went back inside, then began circling the room, combing the walls and corners and ceiling with his eyes. He caught the movement of three delicate spiders, which he crushed at once with his hand. Then he went to the corner where his belongings were stacked, poured some water into the tin bowl, and took his shaving kit and a little mirror out of the trunk. He hung the mirror on one of the nails and contemplated his reflection. Over the past three days, his skin had become darker in some places and redder in others, especially around the eyelids, despite how careful he had been to always wear his cap, which had left a clear mark across his forehead.

He put a little shaving soap on his cheeks and chin, wet the brush with clean water from the bowl, raised it to his face, and began moving it in circles until his skin appeared pure white. Then, he began removing the soap suds with the razor, first from his cheeks, then his neck. By the end of every stroke, suds clung to the razor, the color gradually shifting from white to light brown as they mixed with stubble from his blond beard, which resembled grains of sand. Then he drew the razor along the edge of the bowl, removing the last of the suds, which slowly slid down the bowl until they reached the water's surface, where they floated and gently began to dissolve.

After he finished shaving, he carried the bowl of dirty water outside and poured it onto the sand away from the entrance, then went back into the hut and closed the door behind him, though not all the way, allowing a degree of light to creep in behind him. He poured water from the jerry can into the bowl once more, undressed, and removed the bandage without looking at the bite, which was now infected, though no longer pulsating with pain. He began to wash himself inside the hut, again avoiding bathing with the rest of the soldiers.

First he dipped the towel in the bowl, rubbed it with a bar of soap, then wiped his face, neck, and ears. He rinsed the towel and wiped his stomach and as much of his back as he could reach, before rinsing it again and moving to his arms and armpits, then to his legs, wiping the area surrounding the bite on his thigh very carefully, without looking at it. Despite this, bile rose in his throat, so he quickly looked up and breathed deeply and slowly.

After wiping down his groin, he washed the towel thoroughly with soap and hung it on the wall, then went back to the bed and lay down, leaving his wound unbandaged. After a short while he got up again, walked over to the trunk in the corner, and took out a new roll of gauze, cotton, and antiseptic. He poured some antiseptic onto the cotton and hastily cleaned the wound, then wrapped the gauze around his leg without pulling it tight. He returned to the trunk, put the antiseptic back, and bent over the kit bag lying next to it. He took out a set of clean clothes, which gave off a fresh smell, albeit faint, and the scent slithered into his nose and coiled there briefly before dissipating.

The clean, dry fabric chafed against his skin as he dressed, and then he continued scouring the walls, floor, and ceiling with his swollen eyes, occasionally blinking. Around him, the sense of calm was complete. After he put on his boots, he headed to the half-closed door, opened it wide, and stood there, staring at the view that extended before him. Most of what he saw was sky, with the sun to the western edge, then the sand, tents, and second hut, and a short distance from it was the dog, lying with its head on its front paws, staring at the door of the second hut, which was closed and guarded by a soldier sitting nearby.

* * *

The dog sprang up on all fours and began to bark when he approached the second hut, but he did not look at it. Instead he turned to the guard and ordered him to open the door. He stepped into the hut, accompanied by sunlight, but when it failed to conquer the darkness inside he immediately turned around and told the guard, who stood outside waiting, to bring the girl and follow him.

He had taken a few steps when the dog started barking again, so, without turning back, he slowed his pace and lowered his gaze to his shadow on the sand, which crept weightlessly before him as he crossed the camp to the water tank, while the guard went to carry out his orders. It was afternoon.

When he reached the tank, he turned to the guard, who had the girl by the arm and was walking behind him, followed by the dog. He ordered him to stay there, then glanced at the soldiers' tents. Several of them had left their places in the tents' shade and were also making their way to the water tank, staring at the scene unfolding before them. He ordered the first soldier his eyes landed on to fetch a hose and connect it to the tap, and the soldier immediately set off toward the supply dump at the center of camp. The crowd of soldiers who had gathered in a circle around them silently shifted their gazes from him to the girl, while he observed the dog standing nearby, then turned his gaze to the tents, which were racing the sand dunes toward the pale blue sky.

The soldier returned a short while later carrying a hose wrapped around his arm in equal-sized rings and walked straight to the tank to fit one end onto the tap. He told the soldier to bring him the other end, and the man tossed the coil to the ground so that it would obediently follow him over the sand as he walked away from the tank. And as soon as the soldier handed him the hose, he flew at the girl, stripping the black scarf from her head with his left hand, then he brought both hands to the collar of her dress and, still holding the hose in his right, pulled in opposite directions, releasing a sharp sound that cleaved the silence. He then circled around the girl, unwinding the torn dress from her body, and threw it as far as he could, along with the other scraps of clothing she was wearing. A mixture of odors had collected in their weave: the scent of manure, a sharp smell of urine and genital secretions, and the sour stench of old sweat overpowering new. The air gradually filled with all these pungent smells, some of which still clung to the girl's body, forcing him at times to turn his head to avoid breathing the air around her. Finally he took a few steps back and told the soldier who had brought him the hose and who was still standing nearby to turn on the tap.

A few moments later, a stream of water pushed through the hose, making it heavier in his hand; then suddenly he took his finger from the nozzle and the water rushed over the sand, seeping down through the grains and turning it the same color as the sand reclining in the shade. Quickly, he aimed the nozzle at the girl, and water began pouring over her body.

He went on spraying her, arching his body to avoid the water flying in every direction, and circled around her, aiming the water first at her stomach, then her head, her back, her legs, and her feet, where grains of sand stuck to her skin, then at her torso again. And after he had drenched every part of her body, he covered the nozzle with his thumb, then turned to the crowd of soldiers circled around him and told the first one his gaze fell on to bring him a bar of soap immediately.

The soldiers glanced at each other and at the girl curled into a ball on the sand, shivering, until the soap arrived, and it slid from the soldier's palm, to his palm, to the sand at her feet. He pointed at the bar of soap with his right hand, which was still holding the hose, while his left hand circled around his head and chest. She remained motionless, and a few stifled laughs came from the direction of the soldiers. Then, staring directly into her eyes, he shouted at her, ordering her to pick up the soap, and immediately the soldiers' laughing and mutterings fell silent, leaving only the dog's panting, which chafed against the air. Slowly, the girl reached her hand toward the soap and picked it up. Water trickled down her body. She straightened slightly and began moving the soap in circles over her head, then her chest, which was soon covered with a fine layer of white suds, concealing, for a moment, the brown of her skin. As she did, he looked down at the circle of wet sand besieging her. The water had not escaped very far; the sand immediately around her feet had soaked it all up. When he raised his gaze back to the girl, soap suds were covering most of her body, especially her front. He took his thumb off the hose, and water gushed through it again, but he quickly pinched the nozzle with his thumb and forefinger, making the water shoot harder and further, and aimed it at the girl.

He began removing the soap from her body, sometimes pushing suds to areas the bar had not reached by pointing the hose and aiming the stream of water flowing from it. After removing most of the soap from her body, he covered the nozzle of the hose with his thumb and ordered the tap to be turned off, not directing his words at anyone in particular. While commotion rose around him again, the dog continued standing there, tense and alert, its tongue trembling as it panted nervously. Suddenly, he called to the soldier heading to the tap and told him to wait a little, then he took his thumb off the hose and directed the stream at the dog. But as soon as the water struck it, it ran away, causing the soldiers to laugh loudly, and he smiled, then again ordered the soldier to turn off the tap. The water stopped and he tossed the hose onto the sand.

Lying nearby, not far from the hose, was the girl's old, ripped clothing, its sun-faded color reminiscent of desiccated plants.

He issued another order that several soldiers competed to carry out, and not much time passed before one of them returned holding a shirt, and another carrying shorts, which he took with his right hand and extended to the girl.

His hand remained suspended, the shirt and shorts dangling from it for some time, until the girl's left hand reached for them, while her right hand tried to cover her front as best she could. The sun, in the meantime, had dried the water on her body, except for droplets scattered across her skin and in the shade of her right breast. His gaze hung there for a moment, then shifted to her hand. It was very close to his, so he quickly opened his fingers, but before her hand could take the clothes they dropped to the sand.

* * *

By putting on her new uniform, the girl resembled the members of the platoon standing around her, apart from her long, curly hair. He scanned the group of soldiers until he spotted the medic, whom he charged with a new task: to sterilize and cut her hair, in order to prevent lice from spreading in the camp. The medic left the crowd accompanied by a soldier, and they returned a few minutes later, the medic carrying a bag and a small chair, and the soldier carrying a jerry can that gave off a smell of gasoline. The medic placed the chair on the ground and set the bag beside it, then turned to the girl, took her by the arm, and led her toward the chair, pressing down on her shoulders to make her sit. He bent over his bag, removed a pair of gloves, and nimbly donned them, then gestured for the soldier to bring him the jerry can. The medic took it and began pouring gasoline over the girl's hair until it was completely soaked. Then he set the jerry can aside and patiently began to rub her scalp, focusing on the roots of her hair, behind the ears and above her nape. The medic took a comb and scissors from his bag and looked up at him, asking how short her hair should be cut. To the ears, he replied. The medic partitioned her hair with the comb, revealing a strip of her pure white scalp to the sun.

The soldiers watched the girl's hair fall silently to the sand around her. Meanwhile, the guard had grabbed the dog, and a second soldier was now rubbing gasoline he had poured from the jerry can into its light yellow fur. As they worked, a shiver passed through the officer's body, lasting for several seconds despite the searing rays of the afternoon sun that shone directly onto them.

The medic soon finished cutting her hair, and then he sterilized the scissors, comb, and chair. Another soldier gathered the hair strewn across the sand, collecting it in a piece of cloth which he rolled into a ball and added to the pile of her tattered clothes, and on the officer's orders, set the whole thing on fire.

Far from the flames that consumed her clothes, a few tiny black ringlets of hair remained scattered across the sand.

* * *

The girl was brought back to the second hut, and the guard and dog each returned to their stations in front of the door, while the crowd of soldiers gradually disbanded, withdrawing to the shade of the tents, and leaving him, his deputy, and three division sergeants behind in conversation. They needed to be more cautious from now on, and additional groups of soldiers had to be stationed on high alert around the camp in case some Arabs launched an attack on them in revenge for the morning's operation. As for the girl, he would take her to the central command office himself or leave her in an Arab area at the first opportunity; they could not keep her here for long. In the meantime, they would let her work in the camp kitchen.

After this, he left the group and headed to the main gate, and from there toward the hills in the west to carry out a quick survey patrol. But cramps in his limbs prevented him from going very far, so he sat down on a nearby hill and went on surveying the barren yellow scene. Aside from the occasional sound of soldiers laughing or calling to each other, silence enveloped him. Then some images materialized before his eyes; the camel fallen on the sand, a clutch of grass ripped up by the roots, and then the girl.

* * *

He must have dozed off for some time. He opened his eyes and looked to his right, back toward the camp, while his left hand reached for the swelling on his thigh, feeling it through his pants. Then he stood up and began to walk toward the sun, away from the camp. The sun was now very close to the line of the horizon.

He continued walking west until the sounds coming from the direction of the tents diminished and he could no longer hear them. And when they had completely disappeared, he collapsed on one of the dunes, panting and with bile rising in his throat. He took a few deep breaths, his eyes clinging to the desert as it extended west, and avoided looking directly at the disc of the sun. The heat was still intense, even though the hour was nearing six p.m.

Then the sun vanished behind the hills and a breeze swept in, lightening the heavy air, as a star glimmered hesitantly above the horizon to the east. He got to his feet with some effort and turned back toward camp, guided by the evening star, and the further he walked, the louder the dog's barking became as it echoed through the space. All the while, darkness trickled through the sky, deepening its shade of blue. Evening, August 12, 1949.

* * *

The dog was still barking when he returned to the camp. He headed straight for the second hut, and as he drew closer it barked even louder. He asked the soldier on guard if everything was all right, and the guard answered yes. Suddenly, the door opened and the girl stepped out, crying and babbling incomprehensible fragments that intertwined with the dog's ceaseless barking.

And in that moment after dusk, before complete darkness

fell, as her mouth released a language different to theirs, the girl became a stranger again, despite how closely she resembled all the soldiers in camp.

To the right of the hut, the guard stood motionless and hung his head, avoiding the gaze of his superior, who indifferently shook his head.

* * *

That evening, he ordered them to prepare a special meal to celebrate the success of their morning patrol, after so many fruitless ones before it. At exactly eight o'clock, as the last soldier sat down to the dinner table, he stood up and greeted the platoon, then commended them for their role in defending and protecting the area.

"The south is still in danger, and we must do everything we can to stand our ground and remain here, otherwise we will lose territory. We must not hesitate to devote all the strength and vigor of spirit that we have to building this part of our infant state and protecting and preserving it for future generations. This requires that we go after the enemy, instead of waiting for him to appear, for 'If someone comes to kill you, rise and kill him first.'

"We cannot stand to see vast areas of land, capable of absorbing thousands of our people in exile, remain neglected; we cannot stand to see our people unable to return to our homeland. This place, which now seems barren, with nothing aside from infiltrators, a few Bedouins, and camels, is where our forefathers passed thousands of years ago. And if the Arabs act according to their sterile nationalist sentiments and reject the idea of us settling here, if they continue to resist us, preferring that the area remain barren, then we will act as an army. No one has more right to this area than us, after they neglected it and left it abandoned for so long, after they let it be seized by the Bedouins and their animals. It is our duty to prevent them from being here and to expel them for good. After all, Bedouins only uproot, they do not plant things, and their livestock devour every bit of vegetation that lies before them, reducing, day by day, the very few green areas that do exist. We, however, will do everything in our power to give these vast stretches the chance to bloom and become habitable, instead of leaving them as they are now, desolate and empty of people.

"And it is here, in particular, that our creativity and innovation will be tested, once we succeed in turning the Negev into a flourishing, civilized region and a thriving center of learning, development, and culture, as we have done in the northern and central regions. For although it now seems completely arid, these expanses of desert will gradually recede with the planting of trees, and as our people engage in agricultural and industrial ventures, which will enable them to live here. But to realize all this, we must first conquer this area's fiercest and most destructive enemies and protect it as best as we can. And our presence here is the first step toward fulfilling this vision.

"In this desolate, uninhabited place, we are taking part in a battle for the survival of the south. Therefore, we are fulfilling not only a military mission, but a national one as well. We must not let the Negev remain a barren desert, prey to neglect and misuse by Arabs and their animals.

"And here, let me remind you of the phrase we found when we arrived here, on that partially-destroyed wall: 'Man, not the tank, shall prevail.'"

* * *

Near-empty plates and cups littered the tables as the party came to an end, while the soldiers were still immersed in conversation and vociferous laughter, creating a jubilant atmosphere the camp had not witnessed over the previous days. This was the first time since their arrival that everyone seemed in high spirits; the wine may have played a role too. Although there was not much of it, every soldier managed to have a little to drink that night.

At about half past nine, he stood up again and asked everyone to be quiet. His eyes and face were deep red. He reminded them about the girl they had brought to the camp that day, and said that there were some soldiers who had fooled around with her. A thick silence prevailed, subduing the joyousness that had filled the tent until a moment earlier.

Several seconds passed in which no one uttered a word, and the tension swelled until he spoke again, announcing that he was presenting them with two options for a vote: either they send the girl to work in the camp's kitchen, or they all have their way with her.

For a while the soldiers remained startled. Some looked for a reaction in their comrades' eyes, and others looked away in confusion or suspicion; none of them really knew if he meant what he was saying, if he was laying a trap, or if he was drunk. Then, gradually, separate voices rose, quickly building into a boisterous collective cry in favor of the second option.

The rumble and clamor continued to reign in the tent, as soldiers began enthusiastically planning how they would divide their time with the girl, allocating the first day to soldiers in the first squad, the second day to the second squad, the third day to the third squad, and assigning the driver, the medic, the maintenance team, and the cooks to a separate group with the sergeants and squad commanders, corporals, and the officer.

Finally, before taking his seat again, he said in a loud, clear voice that if any of them touched the girl, they would hear from this, and he gestured at the gun resting to his right.

* * *

After dinner, he went straight to the second hut, where he told the guard to bring the girl and follow him, and he headed to his hut, followed by the guard and the girl, who were in turn followed by the dog. On the way there, he passed by the supply dump in the middle of the camp, and appeared a few moments later with a folding bed, which the guard rushed to carry for him.

When they arrived at his hut, he took the folding bed from the guard and brought it inside, while the others waited outside. After a moment a lantern's glow, then the noise of furniture being moved around the room, reached them.

He soon reappeared and told the guard to put the girl by the bed on the left side of the room while he remained in the doorway, staring into the darkness taking shape around him, permeated with the sound of the dog panting. Stars were scattered in their infinite numbers across the clear night sky, but they seemed smaller and less brilliant than the nights before, like the grains of sand strewn across the threshold, which glittered in the soft lantern light emanating from inside. He did not turn to the guard who now had emerged and was standing behind him, but when he finally turned around and saw him, the officer's movements betrayed a slight surprise. Before leaving, he ordered the guard to remain in his position by the door and prevent anyone from entering the hut. He would be back in an hour at most.

He descended the small sandy slope leading to the tents, where the soldiers' low conversations dissipated into the vast darkness. When the sand leveled out, he turned right toward the main gate, and as he passed through it, he continued walking toward the nearby hills, on a quick patrol around the camp.

When he had finished inspecting the area and returned to where he started, he squatted on the sand with his back to the camp, facing the low, undulating hills that swelled in every direction, their deep blue shapes incredibly still. The distant, recurrent noises he had heard over the previous nights had disappeared, and the soldiers' chatter had died down now too. Suddenly the darkness intensified and he turned his swollen, bulging eyes back to the camp. The light that had been shining from the mess tent until a moment earlier had been extinguished; the men had finished cleaning up from the festive dinner. He stood, brushed off the sand that clung to him, and walked back to the camp.

The guard was sitting by the door to his hut, exactly where he had left him. The dog lay in front of him, resting its head on its front paws. After the guard assured him that everything was all right, he dismissed him, telling him to return at six a.m.

As he opened the door to go inside, cramps seized his limbs and back, forcing his body to arch, but he continued into the hut and reached the table, which he had moved closer to the wall to make room for the second bed, and stood there. The silence was absolute, and it teemed with a strong tangy smell, overpowered by that of gasoline. After a moment, the sound of troubled breathing infiltrated the space too, then the sound of a slight movement in the bed.

He stood motionless for a moment, and then his hand managed to guide itself to the lantern on the table and light it. Instantly the room's new shape appeared; the table and chair had been moved and the second bed added, and their shadows traced new shapes across the walls and floor.

He began conducting his thorough inspection of the room. First, the posts of his bed, then the edges of the trunk, and behind the kit bag and his other belongings, then the corner to the left of the door, and the door, the posts of the second bed, and the chair legs and the table, then another corner of the room, the floor and the walls, the ceiling, including every corner, and in one a small spider with a huge shadow appeared. He pulled over the chair, climbed onto it, crushed the spider, then stepped down, dragged the chair back, and sat down. He took off his boots and pushed them under the chair, then stood up, took off his clothes, and placed them on the back of the chair. He walked over to the trunk, removed the bottle of ointment and a new bandage, and carried these with him to the bed, where he sat down on the edge and began removing the bandage from his thigh. But before he could clean the bite and apply some ointment to it, the cramps in his body grew so intense that he could no longer move. He dropped the ointment and bandage next to him on the bed and walked over to the lantern, with an effort that was reflected on his face, and extinguished it. Darkness invaded the hut again. He eased himself onto the bed, lay down on his back, stretched out, and fell asleep.

* * *

He woke up to his own shallow breathing. The heat in the room was intense and the air was dry. He lay still for some time. Any movement could provoke cramps again, which could bring on a sharp headache. He closed his eyes and tried to slow his breathing, but it soon became strained. The dim space was still steeped in a tangy smell emanating from the corner that the girl occupied, and the closed door and low ceiling made it all the more pungent and suffocating. He could not leave the hut to escape the smell. He had to stay with the girl until six a.m., and it was still not yet half past three. He turned onto his right side, then rolled to his left, facing the wall and with his back to the girl. Again, images of events from the day and the previous night assailed him, pushing sleep far away. And again, he opened his eyes.

* * *

He woke up. He was in exactly the same position as when he had fallen asleep, his body facing the wall. He rolled onto his back and stretched out. A faint rustling sound came from the corner occupied by the second bed, as the girl wrapped her arms around her legs. He stared at the ceiling, where pale light trickled down through cracks in the roof. It was past four a.m. now, and she was still awake. He turned to face the wall again, while the dawn light gently eased the room's thick shadows and the heat retained by the air.

* * *

Suddenly, a wave of darkness flooded the hut; it seemed as if time were ebbing back into night instead of advancing toward day. Then a second wave engulfed him, this time of cold, so he pressed his hands between his thighs and curled his body toward the wall. He began to shiver. After a while, he took his trembling hands from between his legs and gripped his belly; the stomachache had returned.

His body continued to shiver, then began shaking violently, and the bedsprings beneath him started to squeak. He pushed his trembling legs out of bed and onto the floor, then managed to stand, and his bed fell silent. He stood there quivering, hugging his body and trying to warm himself, while his feet began absorbing the chill from the floor. It was at its coldest in these hours before dawn, making him shiver even harder. Then the sound of movement rose from her bed again.

After several moments, he approached the second bed, which let out an abrupt squeak. His leg touched the cold metal edge, and the sound of his tremulous breathing mingled with the tense breaths that emanated from the corner where the girl was huddled. And just as he was about to press his body into the bed, her scream filled the room, followed instantly by the dog's howls outside, so he pounced on her, his hand searching for her mouth to shut it. At that she clamped down hard with her teeth and bit him. He quickly pulled his hand back, and shoved the other toward her hair, which, slick with gasoline, slid between his fingers, eluding his grip for a moment, but then he brought his left hand back and held her by the throat, closed his right hand into a fist, and flung it at her face. After that the girl did not move. For a while, he stayed where he was, bent over her. Then he leaned closer, bringing his trembling body to lie next to hers and letting his racing heartbeat echo in her chest.

Outside, the dog continued howling, and the brief sound of the bed squeaking slowed, then subsided completely, once his body had warmed up. But the sound of his tremulous breathing still resonated in the dark space of the room, alternating with the dog's barking outside until there came a last desperate howl, followed by the soft shuffling of its paws as it retreated from the door and sank into the sand. A calm descended.

He closed his eyes, then reached his left hand toward the bite and let his fingers wander over the exposed swelling, so gently they hardly touched the skin. He took his right hand, which now bore a ring of tiny indentations from the girl's bite, and let it rest on her leg.

Then a violent shiver stormed through him and he began trembling again, so he turned his whole body and pressed it against the girl's, placing his left hand on her stomach and his right hand under her back. He continued to shiver, with tremors intermittently rippling through his body from his lower back to his wrists, while his heart pounded hard where his chest touched hers, as the soft light of dawn began to reveal her curves. After a while, he lifted his left hand from her stomach and shifted his whole body onto her left side, before pushing his left hand under her shirt to her right breast, curling his palm to match its shape. Then he lifted her shirt above the chest and lay his body on top of hers. And as the heat of her body warmed him, the waves of trembling gradually subsided.

* * *

With his right hand covering her mouth and his left hand clutching her right breast, the bed's squeaking drifted up over the stillness of dawn, then increased and intensified, accompanied again by the dog's howling.

And after the squeaking finally ceased, the loud howling outside the door continued for a long time.

* * *

His right hand was still covering her mouth, her viscous saliva soaking his fingers, when he opened his eyes. He had slept for half an hour perhaps, not more. A brief shiver ran through the fingers sealing her mouth but quickly passed. The shaking had lifted from his body entirely. He stayed in the same position without moving, while she lay motionless beneath him, before he nodded off again.

A short while later he awoke once more. He lifted his torso slightly, then took his right hand from her lips and brought it to his chest, feeling an indentation left by a button on her shirt, which was still pulled up above her chest. She was quiet beneath him, and his left hand still clutched her right breast. He brought his right hand back to her mouth and clamped down firmly again. And as the bed began squeaking, and the dog howled outside, the languid light of dawn extended its cold threads into every part of the room.

* * *

A mix of putrid smells invaded the air in the room, settling deep into his mouth and nose. He could distinguish the smell of gasoline coming from her hair, and it mingled with an intense sour taste that had a faint edge of sweetness which welled up from the base of his stomach, followed by an acrid smell whose sharp burn clawed at the base of his throat. Overpowering this mixture was a cold, rancid smell that emanated from the girl's unconscious face. Then bile started to rise in the back of his throat and over his tongue, and he jumped from the bed, grabbed his shirt and pants from the chair, quickly dressed, and rushed to the door, where thin slivers of light were creeping in through the cracks. He pulled the door open, stuck his head through the frame, and took a deep breath. The dog leapt to its feet the moment the door opened and began howling and circling on the sand, its muted steps as silent as the morning light spreading over the camp.

Dawn had nearly given way to the soft air of morning, while a thin layer of clouds stretched across the eastern sky, obscuring the early rays of the sun, and in its wan light the scene appeared almost gray. His eyes wandered over the camp, where soldiers were stationed at several observation posts. The soldier he had tasked with guarding the girl was standing by the door to the second hut, and he called to him, telling him to come over at once.

When the soldier arrived, he ordered him to go inside and transfer the girl to the second hut, adding that she stank. A moment later, the sound of metal bedposts scraping against the floor emerged, shrill and deafening to the ears, and it grew more piercing as the bed neared the door, then abated when the front posts reached the sand and disappeared into it.

The guard struggled to drag the bed, which kept sinking into the sand with every step, until another soldier came to help.

The dog accompanied them as they carried the bed, striding alongside the girl, who remained unconscious, her body jostling to the rhythm of the soldiers' movements.

He went back into his hut. The air still smelled putrid and brought bile to his throat again, so he quickly turned around and stepped outside. He stood by the doorway breathing in the clean air, as his eyes tracked the soldiers carrying the bed and the dog following them. When they reached the second hut, they set it down in front of the door. The guard walked to the water tank and turned on the tap, letting water rush into a bucket placed carefully underneath. After a moment, the soldier turned off the tap and carried the bucket back to the second hut. As soon as he got there, he poured the water onto the girl's motionless body; some splashed near the dog, which darted away, and some splattered onto the sand, which as usual refused to let the water travel across it, and instead greedily sucked the moisture down into its depths. The water left behind small patches of clotted sand that would quickly disappear as the gentle morning sunlight from the east began to filter through the gauzy clouds, which would also soon vanish. The two soldiers dragged the bed into the second hut, then emerged and closed the door. He went back into his hut too, shutting the door behind him.

But the putrid smell was still there, and it forced him back to the door, which he opened halfway, so that the soft light and fresh morning air might enter the room. He began rearranging the furniture, putting it back where it had been. He dragged the table and chair to the center of the room, with an effort visible in his grimace. When he had finished, he went over to the jerry can, poured half of the water it contained into the bowl, and carried that to the table. Then he went back and picked up the towel and the bar of soap, and as he approached the table he brought it to his nose to inhale its scent. He took off his shirt and placed it on the chair, and did the same with his pants. He froze. The swelling on his thigh had burst open, and the bite was now a small crater of decaying flesh, which held a mixture of white, pink, and yellow pus and gave off a sharp, putrid smell.

* * *

As he walked toward the vehicle, a small black bird charted a line through the sky, which turned a deeper shade of blue as the sun moved further from the sandy horizon. When he reached the vehicle, he climbed into the seat behind the steering wheel, started the engine, and set off toward the northwestern part of the Negev.

* * *

Although midday had not yet arrived, it was not long before the heat forced him to stop his patrol. As the sun continued its march toward the heart of the sky, its rays struck the hills more intensely and its heat gave weight to the air.

When he stopped the vehicle's engine, a quiet calm ascended over the plateaus and the sharp smell of gasoline suffused the air, bringing the urge to vomit back to his throat. He stepped down from the vehicle and began walking across the sand, heading west; behind him the sun assailed his back, and before him the horizon rippled nervously under the mirage.

He continued walking until a patch of dry grass appeared between the barren hills off in the distance. He paused a moment, then began heading toward it. The black dots were swirling in front of him; always a few paces ahead, they no longer left his eyesight now. And when he stepped onto the grass, the heavy silence enveloping the space disappeared, replaced by the sound of dry grass brushing against his legs and being crushed under his boots. As he walked, his eyes wandered among the plants that formed the patch, the biggest of which sprouted from massive bulbs.

He threw himself onto the slope of a low hill facing the field of dry grass and stared at the sandy ridges that encircled him on all sides, then at the vehicle parked far off to the northeast. He turned his gaze away from the vehicle and rested it on a hole in the sand to his right, where huge ants were marching to and fro, rearranging grains of sand into new shapes in the wake of their quick movements. He looked back at the patch of dry grass and the sandy, yellow expanses stretching before him. Suddenly, a wave of heat swept over him, spreading through his body like a flame and pushing him down onto the sand. He rested his head on his right palm, then his left hand reached for his cap and pulled it over his forehead, and as it did, the smell of gasoline clinging to his left hand invaded his nose, forcing him to turn his face to the side to avoid it. His nose was now turned toward the sand, and he breathed in the air resting on its surface, which was faintly redolent of something dry.

* * *

He returned to the vehicle, got into the driver's seat, and trained his heavy eyes on the sand dunes, though the sunlight reflecting off them was burning his weary face. He started the engine and pressed his right foot on the gas pedal, but the vehicle did not move; the wheels just spun on the sand. He lifted his foot from the pedal, took a few deep breaths, then pressed it again, and the vehicle lurched forward, heading southeast.

When he arrived back at camp, the dog met him at the gate, howling frantically in his direction. As he stepped out of the vehicle, several soldiers moved away from the second hut, walking in different directions, and then another soldier emerged

47

from the hut, hastily buttoning his pants as he closed the door, which no one was guarding, behind him.

He walked toward the hut, shouting the name of the soldier he had tasked with guarding the girl. As he reached it, the guard's reply came from behind him, but at that moment the door opened and the girl emerged, screaming and sobbing. He turned to the guard, who was now a few steps away, and ordered him to take her back into the hut. The guard rushed to her and began dragging her toward the open doorway, but she tried to resist, turning her face toward the officer, who averted his face to avoid the smell of gasoline lingering in the air behind her. The girl continued sobbing and screaming after she was forced into the hut. When the guard emerged, closing the door behind him, the officer stared, ordering him not to move from his post, then walked off toward his hut.

Meanwhile, the girl's wailing faded into a barely audible weeping, making the dog's howling gradually subside.

* * *

When he entered his hut, the putrid smell, still hanging in the air, immediately assaulted his nose. He left the door open, then took the towel hanging on the nail and began fanning the stagnant air from the corner of the room that the second bed had occupied the night before, trying to push it toward the door, then outside. He kept working to expel the smell from the room until the towel dropped from his hand. He picked it up from the floor, tossed it over the back of the chair, and began combing the room with his eyes from where he stood. After a moment, he pulled the chair to him and sat down, but then he stood up again and headed to the corner where his belongings were. He poured some water from the jerry can into the bowl and removed his shirt, then his shoes and socks, and finally his pants, where some thorns and dry grass had stuck to the fabric. He took the towel, dipped it in the bowl, rubbed it with the bar of soap, and passed it over his face and neck. Then he rinsed it, rubbed it again with the soap, and wiped his chest and arms. He rinsed it, passed the bar of soap over it again, and wiped his armpits. Then he rinsed it, rubbed more soap on it, and wiped his legs, without removing the bandage from his thigh. When he had finished wiping down his entire body, he rinsed the towel once more and hung it where it had been before.

He put the same clothes back on; they still smelled pleasant despite the faint odor of sweat. He carried the bowl outside and poured the water it held onto the sand, brought it back inside, and then headed to the second hut.

The guard and dog were sitting by the door, but as he approached, the dog stood up and began howling, and the guard got to his feet too. He looked at the dog, then at the guard, and ordered him to tell his deputy and the driver to get ready for a quick mission immediately, then to go find a shovel and bring it to the vehicle, where he would be waiting for them.

He stood by the door and fixed his gaze on the dog as the guard left to carry out his orders. The dog had stopped barking and was now turning its head to look around the camp. A moment later, some noise emanated from the command tent, and he looked in that direction. His deputy and the driver emerged from the tent, followed by the guard. As the first two soldiers headed to the vehicle, the guard went to the supply dump near the command tent.

* * *

His deputy and the driver were waiting by the vehicle as the officer walked toward it, directing the girl in front of him with the dog following behind, while the guard ran toward them from the other direction, carrying a shovel.

Meanwhile, a few soldiers stood up from where they had been sitting in the shade of the tents, watching the scene that was unfolding in front of them. A sense of calm permeated the camp, tainted only by the heat of the morning sun as it rose through the sky, until a soldier called to the group standing by the vehicle, asking for his shorts back, which he had given her to wear the previous day.

The vehicle finally set off, and the dog ran after it, trying in vain to keep up. And as it receded into the distance, the dog's barking prevailed over the engine's roar, until eventually it vanished into the dunes.

They had not gone very far from camp when he ordered the driver to stop, adding that they did not have much gasoline. The engine fell silent and the officer got out first, followed by the other men. He ordered the guard to dig a hole two meters long and half a meter wide, in that spot, he said, pointing to a patch of sand that looked no different from any other. Only a few minutes had passed since they had stopped the vehicle when the shovel's blade descended into the spot he indicated; it calmly cleaved the sand, scooping out as much as possible and tossing it as far as the guard's arms and the shovel's handle could reach.

The digging continued in almost perfect silence, aside from the shovel's scraping as it lifted and tossed the sand, together with the sounds of soldiers back in the camp, which arrived from over the hills as vague murmuring, the distance having dispelled the clarity of their voices. Suddenly, a sharp scream tore through the air. The girl was wailing as she ran away, then she fell to the sand before the sound of the gunshot was heard. Silence prevailed again.

Blood poured from her right temple onto the sand, which

steadily sucked it down, while the afternoon sunlight gathered on her naked bottom, itself the color of sand.

He left the guard, who went on digging the hole, and his deputy and the driver who were standing next to him, and returned to the vehicle. He was shivering when the driver approached a moment later and said she might not be dead, they could not leave her like that, it would be better to be sure she was dead. He kept shivering, paralyzed by a tearing pain in his intestines, then finally he moved his mouth and ordered the driver to tell his deputy to do it. A short while later, the sound of six gunshots rang out in space, then silence fell once again. Morning, August 13, 1949.

* * *

The hills of sand parted, revealing the camp once more and the dog running toward them, barking frantically. When the vehicle stopped, it stopped too, but it did not stop barking.

They stepped out of the vehicle, and the deputy sergeant, driver, and guard headed toward the soldiers' tents, and he headed to his hut, followed by the dog that was still howling in his direction. After several paces, he turned and kicked it, and the dog yelped loudly and ran off while he continued walking to his hut. When he entered, he was greeted by a wave of intense heat, accompanied by a trace of the putrid smell.

He went to the corner where his belongings were, picked up the bar of soap, crumbled it into very small pieces between his fingers, and scattered them over the area that had been occupied by the second bed. Then he went back to the corner, picked up the jerry can of water, poured the last of it into the tin bowl, and carried the bowl to the table, then went to his trunk and took out a new bar of soap. He returned to the table, cupped his hands in the water, and splashed some on his face, then took the new bar of soap and worked it into a lather, rubbing it between and over his wet hands, softening its sharp edges. He rubbed the suds over his face, then rinsed it well with the water. A numbing sensation was beginning to seize his body. He slowly dried his face and hands, then went to the bed and lay down, resting his right hand over the edge, where his fingers touched the delicate cold air hidden underneath, away from the heat that weighed heavily in the room.

He had nearly dozed off when his eyes, gazing dimly at the ceiling, caught some movement on his chest, and he jumped and brushed at it, but it was only a button on his shirt that had shifted with his breathing. He resumed staring at the ceiling, inspecting different parts with his eyes, until a light shuffling sound across the floor brushed his right ear.

The dog approached his right hand where it was hanging in the air and began sniffing it. Suddenly, he clamped his hand around its jaws; the dog's stifled barking made his palm vibrate, and the space filled with the sound of its paws slipping on the floor as it tried to flee his grasp. The dog strained against him. And the harder it strained, the more it stumbled and slipped on the floor, the more tremulous its stifled barking became, and the sharper the bed's squeaking, until finally he opened his hand and the dog scrambled across the floor, letting out a loud, desperate howl as it fled.

His right hand hung over the edge of the bed, while his left rested on his chest, still exuding a faint smell of gasoline.

— 2 —

After I had finished hanging the curtains over the windows,
I lay down on the bed. At that moment, a dog on the opposite hill began to howl incessantly. It was past midnight and I
couldn't sleep, despite how thoroughly exhausted I was. I had
spent the whole day arranging and cleaning the house; I dusted
the furniture, swept the floor, and rewashed the bedsheets and
towels and most of the dishes, even though, in principle, the
house was clean before I began cleaning it so thoroughly; the
landlord told me he'd brought in a woman especially. I'd started
renting this house a few days earlier, right after getting my new
job. On the whole, the house is good and the job is good and
my colleagues are nice. But none of this was enough to help
me overcome the anxiety and fear that the dog's endless howling awakened in me that night, not even a little. Regardless,
I realized that when I woke up the next morning, I'd feel an
overwhelming sense of satisfaction, its main source being the
cleanness of the house, and perhaps the curtains hung over its
windows. I had placed my table by the biggest window, where
I would sit every morning and drink my coffee before going to
my new job, and the neighbors and their three children would

pass by and wave to me, all of which would imply that I lived a peaceful life, overlooking a back garden hidden from view.

The borders imposed between things here are many. One must pay attention to them, and navigate them, which ultimately protects everyone from perilous consequences. This grants a person a sense of serenity, despite everything else. There are some people who navigate borders masterfully, who never trespass, but these people are few and I'm not one of them. As soon as I see a border, I either race toward it and leap over, or cross it stealthily, with a step. Neither of these two behaviors is conscious, or rooted in a premeditated desire to resist borders; it's more like sheer stupidity. To be quite honest, once I cross a border, I fall into a deep pit of anxiety. It's a matter, simply put, of clumsiness. Once I realized that I inevitably fail whenever I try to navigate borders, I decided to stay within the confines of my house as much as possible. And since this house has many windows, through which the neighbors and their children can easily see me and catch me trespassing borders even when I'm in my own house, I hung the curtains, although I'll inevitably forget to close them sometimes.

In any case, since I'm always alone when I'm in my house, I'll sit at my table, nowhere else, and that's all the outside world will see of me, to the extent that when a few days pass without me doing so, the neighbor's middle son will tell me he missed seeing me sitting at my table every morning, "working." Indeed, I justify my extended mornings sitting there by telling others that I'm "working." And I usually "work" before going to my new job, which will forever be "new" to me, since I don't know at what point my "new job" should simply become my "job." I often work until late at night, outlasting even the security guard, since I'm often late getting to the office to start my shift, because the dog on the opposite hill usually wakes me up at night, and I don't manage to fall back asleep until dawn, so I wake up late, then get to my new job late. And when none of this happens, I stay in my house until the last hours of morning, sitting at my table "working," but on what exactly?

On the whole, I realize that this might seem exaggerated, but this is due to the issue I previously mentioned, namely my inability to identify borders, even very rational borders, which makes me overreact sometimes, or underreact at other times, unlike most people. For instance, when a military patrol stops the minibus I take to my new job, and the first thing that appears through the door is the barrel of the gun, I ask the soldier, while stuttering, most likely out of fear, to put it away when he's talking to me or asking to see my identity card. At which point the soldier starts mocking my stutter, and the passengers around me grumble because I'm overreacting; there's no need to make things so tense. The soldier isn't going to shoot at us, and even if he does, my intervention won't change the course of things; quite the opposite. Yes, I realize all that, just not in the moment, but rather hours, days, or even years later. That's one example. But this same behavior can be observed in various other situations, from undressing during a security inspection at a checkpoint, to asking an amateur vegetable seller sitting in Ramallah's vegetable market, which is otherwise closed on Fridays, about the price of some wilting lettuce, and being quoted three times the normal price of normal lettuce. Since I lack the ability to evaluate things rationally, situations like these have a severe impact on me; they shake and destabilize me to the point that I can no longer fathom what is permissible and what is not, and I end up trespassing even more borders, worse ones than before. Yet all my fear and anxiety and internal turmoil dissipates when this trespassing occurs within the confines of my solitude. Solitude is so forgiving of trespassed borders; it was only thanks to my time spent alone, sitting at my table in the mornings, "working" on something, that I was able to make my discovery.

By the way, I hope I didn't cause any awkwardness when I mentioned the incident with the soldier, or the checkpoint, or when I reveal that we are living under occupation here. Gunshots and military vehicle sirens, and sometimes the sound of helicopters, warplanes, and shelling, the subsequent wail of ambulances; not only do these noises precede breaking news reports, but now they have to compete with the dog's barking, too. And the situation has been like this for such a long time that there aren't many people alive today who remember little details about what life was like before all this, like the detail about the wilting lettuce in an otherwise closed vegetable market, for example.

So, one morning when I was reading the newspaper, and happened across an article about a certain incident, it naturally wasn't the incident itself that began to haunt me. Incidents like that aren't out of the ordinary, or, let us say, they happen in contexts like this. In fact, they happen so often that I've never paid them much attention before. For instance, on another morning when it was raining, I woke up late, which meant I couldn't sit and "work" at my table in front of the big window; instead I had to go straight to my new job. When I arrived at my stop, and got off the minibus a bit before the clocktower, I found the street empty of people and cars, and I saw a military vehicle stopped in front of al-Bandi grocery. But since there was nothing out of the ordinary in that, I kept walking in the other direction, toward my new job. And when I arrived at the top of the street that leads to my office, a passerby, the only one I had encountered until that moment, pointed out that the area was under curfew, and the army was besieging a building nearby. Nothing struck me as unusual about this either, and I continued on my way. Then, there in the middle of the street, in front of the main entrance to the building where my office is, I glimpsed two soldiers. And by now I've learned my lesson, that I must remain calm and composed in situations like this, and so I waved at them, saying in a clear, confident voice that I worked in the building they were standing in front of. At that, one of them bent his right knee to the ground and propped his left elbow on his other knee, aiming the barrel of his gun at me, and immediately I leapt behind a thorn acacia tree, using its prickly branches to shield myself from gunshots, which, in any event, never came. And while his action, by which I mean him pointing his gun at me, cannot be described as humane, it was enough for me to understand what he meant, and that I had to find another way to my new job. Up until this point, I had not found the situation to be unusual, or not so unusual that I should turn around and go back to my house. So I jumped over the walls and borders dividing the houses and buildings, and I do believe that jumping over borders is fully justifiable in a situation like this, is not it? Anyhow, I carried on in that fashion until I reached the back of the building where I work. And since only three of my colleagues had come to the office that morning, I got to work without anyone disturbing me, carrying out my responsibilities diligently, and very well, until a colleague came into my office and opened the window without my permission, and when I protested, he said the glass would shatter if he did not do so. The army had informed the residents in the area that it was going to bomb one of the neighboring buildings where three young men had barricaded themselves, which is exactly what happened a few minutes later. There was one window this colleague had forgotten to open, and the glass shattered the moment the building was bombed.

Still, the result of him opening the window in my office was unbearable, since right after the explosion, which shook the office a great deal, a thick cloud of dust burst in, some of which landed on my papers and even on my hand, which was holding a pen, forcing me to stop working. I absolutely cannot stand dust, especially that kind, with its big grains that make a shuddersome sound when dusty papers rub against each other, or when one marks on them with a pen. And so only after eliminating every last mote of dust from my office was I able to return to my papers. Here, some might think that my dedication to work reflects a desire to cling to life, or a love for life despite the occupation's attempts to destroy it, or the insistence that we have on this earth what makes life worth living. Well, I certainly cannot speak for anyone else, but in my case it's rather that I am unable to evaluate situations rationally, and I don't know what should or should not be done. All I can do without risking calamitous consequences is work at the office, or sit in my house at my table in front of the big window, which is how I ended up reading that particular article, where the specific thing that caught my attention was a detail related to the date of the incident it described. The incident took place on a morning that would coincide, exactly a quarter of a century later, with the morning of my birth. Of course, this may seem like pure narcissism, the fact that what drew me to the incident, what made it begin haunting me, was the presence of a detail that is really quite minor when compared to the incident's major details, which can only be described as tragic. It's completely plausible, though, for this type of narcissism to exist in someone. It's an innate tendency, one might say, toward a belief in the uniqueness of the self, toward regarding the life one leads so highly that one cannot but love life and everything about it. But since I do not love my life in particular, nor life in general, and at present any efforts on my part are solely channeled toward staying alive, I doubt that a diagnosis of narcissism would fully apply to me here. It's something else, something related more to that inability of mine to identify borders between things, and evaluate situations rationally and logically, which in many cases leads me to see the fly shit on a painting and not the painting itself, as the saying goes. And it is possible, at first glance, to mock this tendency, which could compel someone, after the building next to their office at their new job is bombed, to be more concerned about the dust that was created by the bombing and that landed on their desk than about the killing of the three young men who had barricaded themselves inside, for instance. But despite this, there are some who consider this way of seeing, which is to say, focusing intently on the most minor details, like dust on the desk or fly shit on a painting, as the only way to arrive at the truth and definitive proof of its existence. There are even art historians who make these same claims. All right, they don't exactly claim to notice fly shit on a painting, but they do make a point of focusing on the least significant details, not the most significant ones, in order to determine, for example, whether a painting is an original or a copy. According to them, when art forgers imitate a painting, they pay attention to major, significant details, like the roundness of the subject's face or the position of the body, and these they reproduce precisely. However, they rarely pay attention to little details like earlobes or fingernails or toenails, which is why they ultimately fail to perfectly replicate the painting. Moreover, others claim, based on the same idea, that it is possible to reconstruct something's appearance, or an incident one has never witnessed, simply by noticing various little details which everyone else finds to be insignificant. It's the kind of thing that happens in old fables, like the tale where three brothers meet a man who has lost his camel, and immediately they describe the lost beast to him: it is a white camel, blind in one eye, carrying two skins on its saddle, one full of oil and the other of wine. You must have seen it, shouts the man. No, we have not seen it, they reply. But he does not believe them and accuses them of stealing his camel. So the four men are brought before the court, where the three brothers prove their innocence by revealing to the judge how they were able to describe an animal they had never seen before, by noticing the smallest and simplest details, such as the camel's uneven tracks across the sand, a few drops of oil and wine that spilled from its load as it limped away, and a tuft of its shedding hair. As for the incident mentioned in the article, the fact that the specific detail that piqued my interest was the date on which it occurred was perhaps because there was nothing really unusual about the main details, especially when compared with what happens daily in a place dominated by the roar of occupation and ceaseless killing. And bombing that building is just one example. Even rape. That doesn't only happen during war, but also in everyday life. Rape, or murder, or sometimes both; I've never been preoccupied with incidents like these before. Even this incident in which, according to the article, several people were killed, only began to haunt me because of a detail about one of the victims. To a certain extent, the only unusual thing about this killing, which came as the final act of a gang rape, was that it happened on a morning that would coincide, exactly twenty-five years later, with the morning I was born. That is it. Furthermore, one cannot rule out the possibility of a connection between the two events, or the existence of a hidden link, as one sometimes finds with plants, for instance, like when a clutch of grass is pulled out by the roots, and you think you've got rid of it entirely, only for grass of the exact same species to grow back in the same spot a quarter of a century later. But, at the same time, I realize that my interest in this incident on the basis of a minor detail such as the date on which it occurred is a sign that I'll inevitably end up trespassing borders once again. So, every day since I learned about it, I try to convince myself to forget it entirely, and not do anything reckless. The date on which it occurred cannot be more than a coincidence. Besides, sometimes it's inevitable for the past to be forgotten, especially if the present is no less horrific; that is, until I'm awoken at dawn one morning by the dog barking, followed by the wail of a strong wind. I rush to close all the windows until I get to the big window, through which I see how mercilessly the wind is pulling at the grasses and trees, shaking their branches in every direction, while the leaves tremble and writhe back and forth, nearly ripping off as the wind viciously toys with them. And the plants simply don't resist. They just surrender to the fact of their fragility, that the wind can do what it wishes with them, fooling around with their leaves, passing between their branches, penetrating their boughs, and all the while it carries the dog's frantic barking, tossing the sound in every direction. And again, a group of soldiers capture a girl, rape her, then kill her, twenty-five years to the day before I was born; this minor detail, which others might not give a second thought, will stay with me forever; in spite of myself and how hard I try to forget it, the truth of it will never stop chasing me, given how fragile I am, as weak as the trees out there past the windowpane. There may in fact be nothing more important than this little detail, if one wants to arrive at the complete truth, which, by leaving out the girl's story, the article does not reveal.

The dog's barking continues to echo in the air until the last hours of morning; sometimes the wind carries it closer to me, and sometimes further from me, until I have to leave for my

new job. But before I do, I call the author of the article, an Israeli journalist, and try to pass myself off as a self-confident
person. I introduce myself as a Palestinian researcher, while
trying as hard as possible not to stutter, and explain the reason
for my call. Neither the introduction nor the explanation thrills
him. I ask if he would share with me the documents in his possession which relate to the incident. He replies that everything
he has is there in the article. I add that, even so, I would like to
look at them myself, and he says that if that's what I'd like, I can
go and look for them myself. Where? I ask him. In museums
and archives of the Israeli military and Zionist movements
from the period, and those specializing in the area where the
incident occurred. And where are they? He replies, in a tone
betraying that his patience has nearly expired, that they're in
Tel Aviv and in the northwest Negev. Then I ask him if, as a
Palestinian, I can enter these museums and archives? And he
responds, before putting down the receiver, that he doesn't see
what would prevent me. And I don't see what would prevent
me either, except for my identity card. The site of the incident,
and the museums and archives documenting it, are located
outside Area C, according to the military's division of the
country, and not only that, but they're quite far away, close to
the border with Egypt, while the longest trip I can embark on
with my green identity card, which shows I'm from Area A, is
from my house to my new job. Legally, though, anyone from
Area A can go to Area B, if there aren't exceptional political or
military circumstances that prevent one from doing so. But
nowadays, such exceptional circumstances are in fact the norm,
and many people from Area A don't even consider going to
Area B. In recent years, I haven't even gone as far as Qalandiya
checkpoint, which separates Area A and Area B, so how can I
even think of going to a place so far that it's almost in Area D?

Even the people from Area B cannot do that, and probably also those from Area C, including people from Jerusalem, whose very existence constitutes a security threat if they utter a word of Arabic outside their areas. They're permitted, of course, to be in Area A, as are residents of Area B, who frequently visit it, and sometimes move there, despite the fact that it's tantamount to a prison now. At my new job, for instance, in addition to people, like me from Area A, many of my colleagues are from other Areas, all very nice people. One day at work, I confide in a colleague from Area C, from Jerusalem, that I need to go to her Area, or perhaps a bit further, to take care of a personal matter; after all, it's not unusual for people from Area A to need to go to Area C for personal matters, and for people from Area C to need to go to Area A for personal matters. On hearing that, my colleague offers to lend me her blue identity card, since we're all brothers and sisters in the end, and we look similar too, at least in the eyes of the soldiers at the checkpoint. Besides, they don't closely inspect women in the first place, so they'll never notice the difference between me and the photo on her identity card. They hardly look at the people standing at the checkpoint anyway, given their contempt, and what's more, people typically look different from the photos on their identity cards, which could have been taken when they'd just turned sixteen. Honestly. Yes, I can easily use her identity card, do what I need to do and return it when we arrive at work at the beginning of next week. No rush at all. And she'll spend the weekend in Ramallah with friends. Of course, if I'm discovered, I'll say that I stole the identity card from her bag, so as not to implicate her. At any rate, I have to be cautious. And I'll certainly make every effort not to be reckless. So, on the afternoon of the last day of the working week, I stop by her office, borrow her identity card and head to a car rental company to rent a car with a yellow number plate, without which one cannot travel to areas beyond Area C. But as I'm about to sign the agreement it becomes clear that I need a credit card, which I don't have. And because I don't want to further burden that colleague, I call another colleague from my new job and ask for his help. He comes to the rental office right away and rents a car for me using his credit card, after listing me on the agreement as an additional driver, as the company employee advises us, and then I get the key. Really, my colleagues are so nice. And now I don't see any reason that would prevent me from embarking on my mission to discover the complete truth about the incident, except that, as soon as I sit down behind the steering wheel of the little white car I've just rented, and turn the key to start the engine, what appears to be a spider begins spinning its threads around me, tightening them into something like a barrier, impenetrable if only because they're so fragile. It's the barrier of fear, fashioned from fear of the barrier. The checkpoint. I've often heard that today, Saturday, is the worst and most difficult day to cross through the Qalandiya checkpoint. Not only is everyone from Jerusalem coming to Ramallah, to buy fresh vegetables from the market there, or to take care of personal matters, but the soldiers are in a vindictive mood, resentful of everyone passing through the checkpoint, everyone who obliges them to work on what should be their weekend, Saturday, the day on which God Himself rested. In any case, Israeli museums and archives are all closed on Saturday for the same reason, which means that I cannot embark on my research immediately anyway. Not today, at least. So I drive the little white car back to my house, where I'll have the opportunity to reconsider my undertaking; maybe I'll finally stop chasing after these reckless ideas, with their inevitably perilous consequences, and rid myself of the conviction that I can un-

64

cover any details about the rape and murder as the girl experienced it, not relying only on what the soldiers who committed it disclosed, as the author of that article did. This type of investigation is completely beyond my ability. And the fact that the girl was killed twenty-five years to the day before I was born doesn't necessarily mean that her death belongs to me, or that it should extend into my life, or that it should be my duty to retell her story. As a matter of fact, I'm the last person who could do that, because of all my stuttering and stammering. In short, there's absolutely no point in my feeling responsible for her, feeling like she's a nobody and will forever remain a nobody whose voice nobody will hear. Besides, people have to deal with enough misery in the world today; there's no reason to go searching for more and digging into the past. I should just forget the entire thing. But then, as soon as darkness spreads into every corner of the house, I'm racked by the dog's howling again; it robs me of sleep until the dawn hours, when I finally nod off, and then wake up late, quickly drink my coffee, grab all the maps I have in the house, and leave. At the far end of the backyard, I find the little white car waiting for me, rays of sunlight drenching the front windshield, and when I open the door and get in, a tender warmth like I haven't felt for a very long time embraces me, soothing my frightened, sleepless self. I start the engine, then head toward the entrance gate where I stop, waiting for the right moment to turn onto the street, as the sound of the right indicator pervades my pounding heartbeats. To the right, then. I haven't gone right, not even on foot, for years. I notice that some landmarks on either side of the road have remained the same since the last time I passed through the area, like the wheat mill in Kufer Aqab, and across from it Abu Aisha's butcher shop in Semiramis, then the row of dusty cypress trees that conceal the Qalandiya Vocational

Training Center building, opposite the camp entrance. Many other features have changed, however, which makes the drive feel unfamiliar. There are far more speed bumps and potholes in the road now, which I try to avoid as best as I can, exactly as the cars in front of me are doing, and the cars behind me too, until I come to a halt a bit past the entrance to the Qalandiya camp, at the end of a line of cars waiting to cross the checkpoint. I immediately raise my gaze to the rearview mirror, trying to evade the fear that the sight of the checkpoint ahead will prompt, when I discover that I'm no longer last in the line of cars. There are at least seven cars behind me now, preventing me from changing my mind and turning around. I take a deep breath and look to my left, where I see a car tire shop. And to my right, a big dump site. The dump site is new, and so is the Wall behind it. In the past, there was a chain-link fence topped with barbed wire here, which once let passersby see the runway at Qalandiya Airport as it extended toward the horizon. Now it is the Wall that extends to the horizon, covered by all sorts of graffiti including quotes from the Code of Hammurabi, a telephone number for a cooking gas cylinder vendor and a painting by Banksy. This is the first time I've seen the graffiti in real life, although I've seen them in newspapers and magazines before, sometimes with important people standing in front of them. By the time the line of cars moves forward a couple of meters, I've studied all the slogans and paintings on the Wall, where hardly any spot remains bare, and have fended off large numbers of children trying to sell me things I haven't any need for. The last one is a little girl with tousled hair, a brown face and mucus running from her nose, who is selling chewing gum. I open my bag, take out a tissue, and offer it to her, asking her to wipe her nose, and immediately she snatches it from my hand and disappears from sight. Then, even before fear can seize me, several children reappear, this time trying to sell me tissues. I ignore them by gazing at the view to my right; specifically, at the new dump site with its endless jumble of colors. Not much can be excavated and reused from the folds of this dump site. Indeed, what ends up here is the very essence of garbage; elsewhere, empty cans of food sit on balconies and stairways in houses, sprouting plants of various kinds, or sit on hobs with boiling water inside, while empty bottles line refrigerator shelves, filled with cold water to quench people's thirst in this intense heat. Leftover food is set before chickens or cows at the end of the day, then given to the dogs guarding them, until the cats finish it off. Newspaper pages, after performing an additional role covering tables or floors, shielding the surfaces from overflowing plates of food, are eventually devoured in the ovens' fire, along with any cardboard boxes not used to store as many potatoes, onions, and garlic heads as they can, not to mention bottles of oil and pickled olives and other such pantry supplies. And, finally, plastic bags keep fulfilling their duty of holding all kinds of bits and pieces, until, in their final act, they're eventually used to hold garbage. Only two cars have crossed by the time the girl returns, and she chases away the children who stuck alongside the car in her absence, pulling me out of my dump site reverie. With a clean nose now, she picks up where she'd left off, begging me to buy chewing gum from her. I contemplate her face then her skinny body, and glimpse the edge of the tissue, which she's shoved into her little pants pocket. It appears that she plans to keep using it until there's not a clean spot left. I raise my eyes to her face, and repeat what I told her earlier, that I don't like chewing gum. But my words may as well be dust, and she keeps begging me to buy chewing gum from her. I respond that I'm more stubborn than she is, and that I won't buy any chewing gum from her no matter how hard she tries, but my words have no apparent effect; she keeps begging me to buy chewing gum from her, while shifting her gaze from my bag to my clothes, then to the inside of the car. Finally, I tell her that she should be in school, not selling chewing gum at the checkpoint. And only when she replies that it's the summer holiday am I sure she's not deaf or slow. Yes, that's right, I had forgotten. Then she goes back to begging me to buy chewing gum from her. I ask about her marks in school. Enthusiastically, she tells me they're good, before repeating her request that I buy chewing gum from her. I ask her what she does with the money she earns from selling chewing gum, if she gives it to her parents, for instance, and she says of course not, she keeps it for herself. I ask how she's going to spend it. She tells me she's going to buy herself presents during the festivities, then goes back to begging me to buy chewing gum from her. I search for my wallet in my bag, take out a few coins, and offer them to the little girl, adding that I don't want any chewing gum. She takes the money, tosses two packs of chewing gum onto the passenger seat next to my bag and runs away. And only now do I realize that I've come quite close to the checkpoint, so close in fact that I can see a soldier examining somebody's papers, and a bolt of pain strikes my heart, then numbness spreads through my body, as the spider of fear crawls across my skin, slowly paralyzing me. I look around frantically, hoping to see the little girl, begging for her to come back, for her company to ease the fear that's sweeping through me, but she's vanished, so instead I fix my gaze on the people waiting to go through the checkpoint on foot, watching as they pass behind the narrow metal bars of the turnstiles one by one, while I try to take deep, slow breaths. These are the lucky ones, lucky enough to pass through the checkpoint, even if they're forced to stand and wait; they're allowed to move from one Area to another whenever they want, without needing to borrow an identity card from their nice colleague at their new job. Then I yawn. I'm completely exhausted, since I barely slept last night. I'm so tired of my reckless behavior and of the state I get myself into, the fear, anxiety, and agitation. It'll be a disaster if they discover what I'm doing, the consequences are so enormous I can hardly imagine them, but if what I'm doing isn't discovered, I will go straight back to my house, right after the checkpoint; yes, it's the only way to put an end to this state I'm in. I promise myself this then I yawn again, and in the middle of my yawning a soldier approaches the car. I watch my hand as it extends the blue identity card toward him. The two packs of chewing gum are still sitting on the seat next to me. The brand is called "Must," made by the Sinokrot company in al-Khalil. I turn my head, stare straight ahead, and see nothing. Then the soldier hits the roof of the car as if to wake me up. I'm alert. He gives me back the identity card and orders me to move. And I move. Forward. More. And more, since I'm afraid of turning around right away, or else the soldier and all the security forces at the checkpoint will notice me. But the road past the checkpoint is blocked by the Wall, as is the road to the left. As such, my only choice is to turn right, where there's a narrow road stretching off into the distance, one I've never taken before, and I'm not sure if I should, but I let the car keep going, onto this road, where to the right is the Qalandiya Airport runway, running parallel to the road, and to the left is empty land, intersected here and there by narrow roads, and I don't dare take any of them, but then I quickly regret the decision not to when another checkpoint appears in front of me. Damn! Fear crushes my heart, and I'm gripped by a strong desire to sleep. And just as I approach the checkpoint and slow down, I let out a powerful yawn, opening my mouth as wide as it can go. I rush to cover it with my hand, and the soldier waves back at me, gesturing for me not to stop, so I keep going, until I arrive at an intersection with several signs in Hebrew and Arabic and English, including one pointing to the left, toward "Jerusalem (al-Quds)," and one pointing to the right, toward "Tel Aviv—Yafo." I turn right. After about a hundred meters, I pull over to the side of the road to catch my breath. My body is trembling. I try to calm down, but I cannot calm down; fear has settled into every part of my body, making it feel practically weightless. Oh, how pitiful I am. I don't know where I am, and if I stay here for long it will start to look suspicious. I take the maps I brought with me out of my bag and spread them over the passenger seat and across the steering wheel. Among these maps are those produced by centers for research and political studies, which show the borders of the four Areas, the path of the Wall, the construction of settlements, and checkpoints in the West Bank and Gaza. Another map shows Palestine as it was until the year 1948, and another one, given to me by the rental car company and produced by the Israeli ministry of tourism, shows streets and residential areas according to the Israeli government. With shaking fingers, I try to determine my current location on that map. I haven't gone far.

Despite that, there is no going back now.

I take a deep breath. Well, no going back now, not after crossing so many borders, military ones, geographical ones, physical ones, psychological ones, mental ones. I look back at the Israeli map, searching for the first location I wish to head to. It's a medium-sized black dot, not far from where I am now, crowned with the word "Jaffa" written in small but thick English letters. There are a few military museums and archives there, where, as the author of the article had informed me, I can find basic information about the incident. I start trying to determine the best route there, relying on the various maps I have with me. While, in principle, the shortest distance between two points is a straight line, in practice I cannot chart a course like that, not because the roads aren't straight but because, as several maps confirm, there are at least two checkpoints on the shortest route leading to Yafa. And neither the maps I have in my possession nor the ones I don't have indicate the locations of flying checkpoints, or are updated with the ongoing construction of the Wall, which continually leads to more road closures. In fact, it's been years since I've heard anyone mention the road that would take me on the shortest route; for instance, that they witnessed a traffic accident there, or that they bought a box of vegetables from a roadside vendor. It can't have dropped from conversation by chance. Rather, it probably means that no one is able to travel on that road any longer. So if I want to continue with my investigation, and on the safest route possible, it's best to choose the longer but faster road, the one Israelis take to the coast. I start the engine and pull back onto the road, slowly, calmly, and cautiously. A few meters ahead and to the right is the road that once led to Ramallah through the village of Beitunia, which I had taken dozens of times en route to Yafa or Gaza. Now it is blocked, closed off. On its right I can see several eight-meter-high concrete slabs, exactly like the ones used to construct the Wall, and which I've seen around the Qalandiya checkpoint, but here they form what looks like a fortress. "Ofer Prison," the sign on the roadside indicates. I've heard a lot about this prison in recent years, but this is the first time I've seen it. It's relatively new, built in 2002, during the wave of invasions that took place in the spring of that year, when the army rounded up anyone over the age of sixteen and under fifty in public squares and brought them here. Among them was a colleague from my new job, who's very nice, originally from

Rafah. One time at the office, he recalled the smell of freshly poured bitumen which shoved its way into his nose as he slept on the asphalt during the months of his detention. On the other side of the prison is a military base hiding behind a row of cypress trees. In the past one could glimpse tanks and military vehicles lurking inside massive hangars through the dusty cypress trunks, branches, and needles. At the intersection, I turn the car back in the direction of Jerusalem on Road 443; I have to turn right on Highway 50 after that, then another right on Highway 1 toward Yafa. I continue driving on Road 443, still on the alert, and before long I catch sight of another checkpoint ahead; my heartbeats echo in my skull, and something akin to a torn spiderweb dances in front of my eyes. I get closer to the checkpoint. I have to cross it. The soldiers lined up around it do not seem concerned with stopping anyone, probably including me. I shouldn't slow down very much. I must trust that I'll get through. And I do! After the checkpoint, however, my confidence dissipates completely and I'm no longer sure where I am. I can't tell whether I've taken this road before, as I'd thought at first, or not. The road I'd been familiar with until a few years ago was narrow and winding, while this one is quite wide and straight. Walls five meters high have been erected on either side, and behind them are many new buildings, clustered in settlements that hadn't existed before or were hardly visible, while most of the Palestinian villages that used to be here have disappeared. I scan the area with eyes wide open, searching for any trace of these villages and their houses, which were freely scattered like rocks on the hills and were connected by narrow, meandering roads that slowed at the curves. But it's in vain. None of them can be seen any more. The further I drive, the more disoriented I become, until, off to the left, I see another road that has been closed. And at this point I realize that I've taken that road before, dozens of times; it's blocked off now by a mound of dirt and several massive concrete blocks, but it once led to al-Jib villages. I stop the car where the roads intersect, step down, and approach the heap of dirt and concrete blocking it, to be completely sure that it exists and cannot be moved, and that neither my car nor any other car can drive around it. It's pretty, the road to al-Jib, the way it leans left and right, crossing hills dotted with olive trees and little villages wrapped in quiet, to Beit Iksa. I go back to the car, open the Israeli map, and again study the route that Israelis usually take to the coast. So, after descending to the bottom of the valley on Highway 50, one must turn right onto Highway 1, and stay on it for a long time, without turning right or left. I examine the area along Highway 1, which, according to the map, appears to be primarily populated by settlements. The only two visible Palestinian villages are Abu Ghosh and Ein Rafa. I go back and open the map, which depicts Palestine until 1948, and let my eyes wander over it, moving between the names of the many Palestinian villages that were destroyed after the expulsion of their inhabitants that year. I recognize several of them; some of my colleagues and acquaintances originate from there, from the villages of Lifta, al-Qastal, Ein Karem, al-Mallha, al-Jura, Abu Shusha, Siris, Innaba, Jimzu, and Dair Tarif. But the majority of the names are unfamiliar to me, to the extent that they invoke a feeling of estrangement. Khirbat al-Ammour, Bir Ma'in, al-Burj, Khirbat al-Buwayra, Beit Shanna, Salbit, al-Qubab, al-Kanisa, Kharrouba, Khirbat Zakariyya, Bariyya, Dair Abu Salama, Al-Na'ani, Jindas, Hadatha, Abu al-Fadl, Kisla, and many others. I look at the Israeli map again. A very large park called Canada Park now extends over the area where all these villages used to be. I fold the maps, start the engine, and set off toward Highway 50, and encountering no barriers this time, I turn onto the really long highway. And after continuing on it for a while, I start to descend the mountains of Jerusalem, heading, according to the signs, toward the Ben Shemen Interchange, whose original name may have been Beit Susin, named after a nearby village which appears on the map from 1948 and which no longer exists. All that is left, all that hasn't been destroyed, is a single house, and I catch a glimpse of it on my left, surrounded by cypress trees and with grass growing through the stones.

The car cuts through the landscape at high speed. The road is nearly perfectly straight, but even so, I keep glancing at the Israeli map unfurled across the seat next to me, fearing that I may get lost in the folds of a scene which fills me with a great feeling of alienation, seeing all the changes that have befallen it. It's been a long time since I've passed through here, and wherever I look, all the changes constantly reassert the absence of anything Palestinian: the names of cities and villages on road signs, billboards written in Hebrew, new buildings, even vast fields abutting the horizon on my left and right. After a disappearance, that's when the fly returns to hover over the painting. Little details drift along the length of the road, furtively hinting at a presence. Clothes hung out to dry behind a gas station, the driver of a slow vehicle I overtake, a thorn acacia tree standing alone in the fields, an old mastic tree. A few shepherds with their livestock on a distant hill. I look back at the Israeli map for a moment, to check that I should take the Kibbutz Galuyot exit to the right, and a moment later it's announced by several giant signs, just as new high-rise buildings emerge from the horizon. From there, I'll turn left onto Salama Road, where I'll continue toward Yafa, or "Yafo," as the signs directing me there declare, until the horizon materializes as a blue line. The sea!

There it is, in real life, after years of absence, years in which it was nothing more than pale blue on a map. And now the sea, not the signs, begins to lead me toward the city, and as I drive on this bleak road, passing factories and auto repair shops, I cannot resist glancing at its trembling blueness every few seconds, until I almost cause an accident. During a brief glance at its rippling surface under the midday sun, I realize suddenly, but too late, that I'm driving through a red light, into a four-way intersection where each road has three lanes, and that all the cars are jolting to a stop to let me go through. Damn! What did I just do! After I pass through the intersection, I pull over on the side of the road to catch my breath, and a numbness extends into every part of me, making me feel heavy. I'm so clumsy; this is exactly the kind of border I cannot trespass. I can't seem to calm down. But I can't stay here either; my car is still obstructing traffic. I turn back onto the road, and my hands are trembling, they feel weightless now, while my feet barely manage to press the accelerator, the clutch, or the brake, and I make it to the end of the road, turn left, continue for a few meters, not much more, and arrive at my first destination, the Israel Defense Forces History Museum. When I arrive, I find that the parking lot is almost empty, which eases my anxiety, but also makes the task of deciding where to park the car a somewhat difficult endeavor. I'm not sure whether it's better to park in the shade, or as close to the entrance as possible, or in a visible spot to prevent the car from being broken into or stolen, or somewhere no one else wants to park, where it's less likely to be scratched, even a bit. When I finally park, after a not-so-insubstantial moment of hesitation, I put all the maps in my bag, as well as the shirt I'd taken off in the heat, and the two packs of chewing gum from the seat beside me, but not before opening one, taking two pieces of chewing gum, and tossing them into my mouth. Aside from coffee, I haven't had anything to eat or drink since this morning, so at the very least I'll absorb some sugar.

I get out of the car and walk calmly toward the museum entrance, then I cross the threshold into the lobby, heading straight for the ticket desk, when I discover a soldier standing there. He looks up at me with a smile. I walk over to him. He doesn't ask to see my nice colleague's identity card, so I leave it in my bag. I hand him the money for a ticket. And he takes it, gives me the ticket, and tells me I must leave my bag in a locker. That's all. His military uniform must be part of the exhibition. I remove my wallet, and a little notebook and pen so that I can take notes, since photography is prohibited inside, as he also informs me. But I don't have a camera with me anyway. I walk out of the lobby and into an open-air courtyard, which visitors must pass through to enter the sixteen exhibition rooms, as indicated in the brochure which the soldier gave me along with my ticket. When I step into the courtyard, I'm instantly met by a sharp, blinding light reflected toward me by the white gravel covering the ground, which also makes a terrible ear-piercing sound as I walk across it. To be quite honest, I have no more tolerance for gravel than for dust. So I keep walking across the gravel, carefully, trying to keep the sound from growing, and through eyes half-closed against the glare I see silhouettes of several old military vehicles positioned around the courtyard, until eventually I realize that this is the sixteenth and final stop in the exhibition, according to the brochure, meant to be visited after all the rooms inside. I feel a wave of nervousness when I realize that I've wandered in the opposite direction to the route suggested by the museum, which might ruin the whole experience for me, so I immediately head to the first exhibition room. And as soon as my feet cross the threshold, leaving the sticky heat that weighed heavily on the courtyard behind me, shivers rise through my body, in response to the cold air being expelled toward me by the air conditioning. I use my hands, which are still holding my wallet and notebook, to cover my arms, trying to warm them up, since I left my long-sleeve shirt with my bag in the locker. But it's in vain. Shivers grip my body again as I wander through the room, which is completely empty of people, aside from a soldier on guard. I try hard to control my shivering, so as not to attract his attention while wandering leisurely in the room among the displays. In one, I find a map of the south and several telegrams sent between soldiers stationed there in the late forties, filled with heroic and encouraging phrases. But the shivering doesn't stop. I take a deep breath, then turn to look at the guard, who I find staring in my direction. I turn away nonchalantly and keep walking, on toward the second room. There, my shivering gradually fades when I stop in front of a collection of photographs and propaganda films, a few of which, the labels indicate, were produced in the thirties and forties by pioneers of Zionist cinema. The films show Jewish European immigrants in Palestine, focusing on scenes of them engaged in agricultural work, and of cooperative life in the settlements. One film in particular gives me pause. It starts with a shot of a barren expanse, then abruptly a group of settlers in shorts and short-sleeve shirts enter the frame. They start constructing a tall tower and wooden huts, working until these are complete, and the film ends with the settlers gathered in front of the finished buildings, with joined hands, dancing in a circle. In order to watch it again, I rewind it to the beginning. The settlers break the circle, then go back to the huts they've just finished building, dismantle them, carry the pieces off in carts, and exit the frame. I fast-forward the tape. Then I rewind it. Again and again, I build settlements and dismantle them, until I realize that I shouldn't waste any more time here; I have to visit several other rooms and inspect their displays, and there is still a long trip ahead. I continue my tour until I reach the sixth room, where I end up spending more time than in the previous rooms. This display features wax soldiers wearing various kinds of military attire and accessories. According to the labels, most of the items were used during the forties. I notice that military uniforms from that period differ from military uniforms today. Contemporary ones are a dark olive-green, while the old ones were gray and came in two styles, long pants or shorts, each held up by a wide fabric webbing with a leather gun holster, small pouches for magazines, and a place to hang a water bottle. There are different kinds of webbing sets, too, some worn around the waist, others across the chest. The wax soldiers also wear kit bags on their backs and have caps on their heads, some large and others small. As for their boots, these very much resemble the ones worn by soldiers today. In the middle of the room are huge glass cases, inside which are displayed various types of equipment and mess kits used at the time, including small rectangular tin bowls connected to a chain with a spoon, fork, and knife. There are other types of equipment too, such as shaving kits and bars of soap and so on. Next to all this is a little scale model of the tents used for soldiers' quarters, mess halls, and command meetings. I continue to the next rooms, which contain displays that don't deserve much attention, that is, until I reach the thirteenth room. The thirteenth room contains various models of small firearms that were used until the fifties. I circle them apprehensively, contemplating the different sizes and shapes, and the size of the bullets displayed alongside the guns in the glass cases, reading the accompanying explanations attentively, before pausing in front of a Tommy gun. The label explains that this is an example of a US-made submachine gun, developed in 1918 by John T. Thompson, thus the name "Tommy," and widely used during the Second World War by the Allied Powers, especially by noncommissioned officers and patrol commanders, and then in the War of 1948, and subsequently in the Korean War, the Vietnam War, and many others. This weapon excelled, the label adds, at hitting a target even at great distance, while also being effective in close combat. I make a sketch of it in my notebook. I've become bad at drawing. In the old days I used to be able to draw and reproduce shapes very precisely. Now, however, my lines are sharp, agitated, and unsteady, which distorts the weapon I've sketched so that it no longer really resembles the weapon used in the crime on the morning of August 13, 1949. Suddenly, a loud roar rises through the room, and I jump and start shivering again. I leave room thirteen and step into the courtyard before the air conditioner's chill extends over the entire room. In the courtyard, I stumble upon the military vehicles used during that period, which I'd seen when I first entered, and am met by a thick wave of heat and blinding white light for a second time. Against this, the dark green shirt of the soldier on guard, whom I saw in the first room and who is now also wandering around the courtyard, soothes my eyes. But not my mental state. At the first sign of fear, I leave the courtyard, head to the lobby, retrieve my bag from the locker and walk to my little white car, which is still alone in the parking lot. Actually, there's no need for me to spend any more time in this city. Official museums like this really have no valuable information to offer me, not even small details that could help me retell the girl's story. I open my little notebook to study my distorted sketch of the Tommy gun, which looks more like a rotten piece of wood than a lethal weapon. I put the notebook in my bag, then pick up the Israeli map to determine my route to my next destination. I must get on Highway 4, which leads south, then, after Askalan and before Gaza, I'll turn left onto Road 34, then right at Sderot onto Road 232, and I'll continue on that until I reach my next destination. I toss the map onto the seat next to me, take the chewing gum from my mouth, drop it in the car ashtray, and depart.

There are other maps lying under the one I've tossed there, including ones that show Palestine as it was until 1948, but I don't open them this time. I'm acquainted with enough people who are originally from this area to have a sense of how many villages and cities there used to be between Yafa and Askalan, before they were wiped from the earth's face not long ago. Meanwhile, names of cities and settlements appear along the road, as do shapes of houses, fields, plants, streets, large signs, and people's faces; all of this accompanies me on my journey while rejecting me too, provoking an inexplicable feeling of anxiety, until I catch sight of a checkpoint where police are inspecting the identity cards of passengers on a white bus just outside Rahat. There they are! And there is a policeman standing on the side of the road as well, ready to select a vehicle, stop it, and subject it to inspection. My heart beats faster at the base of my throat. I must turn my gaze away. I quickly glance at my bag, then plunge my right hand inside, searching for the packs of chewing gum, and when I find one I take out a piece, toss it into my mouth and begin chewing it, while letting my gaze hang on the ridgeline of the hills scattered on the left side of the road. I have to calm down. Although the car had been moving at ninety kilometers an hour, the closer it gets to the checkpoint, the more it slows down, nearly to a complete stop at the checkpoint itself; I swallow some saliva, still chewing the gum, and just as the car crosses the checkpoint it leaps back up to speed. I take a deep breath when the scene appears in the rearview mirror: the policemen busy examining the identity cards of passengers on the white bus, and another policeman standing nearby, considering the cars passing in front of him, still about to select one and stop it for inspection.

I continue sitting behind the wheel until exhaustion pounces on me again, and I lean my head back. There's much less traffic now, and I have come far enough south that the sandy white hills dotted with small stones have been replaced by hills of yellow sand that look soft to the touch. Scraggy, pale green plants grow on some of the hills, reminiscent of the wilting rotten lettuce the amateur vegetable vendor tried to sell me for three times the price of normal lettuce in Ramallah's closed vegetable market. I decide to stop the car by some fields to rest for a bit. I take the chewing gum from my mouth and deposit it in the ashtray, then close my eyes, hoping to nap in my seat for a few minutes. But I can't manage to fall asleep; I feel as if anxiety is lashing at me, keeping me awake. Eventually, when I've lost all hope of resting, I pick up the maps from the seat next to me. First, I open the Israeli one and try to determine my position, relying on the number that appeared on the last sign I saw along the road. It seems I simply have to drive on a straight course, albeit a short one, and I'll soon reach my next destination, which appears on the map as a small black dot, practically the only one in a vast sea of yellow. Next, I pick up the map showing the country until 1948, but I snap it shut as horror rushes over me. Palestinian villages, which on the Israeli map appear to have been swallowed by a yellow sea, appear on this one by the dozen, their names practically leaping off the page. I start the engine back up and set off toward my target.

I see it from afar, in the heart of the yellow hills, and the narrow asphalt road stretches between me and my destination, where a row of flowers and slender dwarf palm trees leads toward several red brick houses. Nirim settlement. When I reach the barrier gate at the main entrance, I stop the car and remain inside, waiting for someone to come out and inspect me, but nothing of the sort happens. After a while, I drive closer to the metal gate and security booth, but I don't see anyone inside, so I get out of the car and head to the gate. The sun is very strong. I hold onto the bars of the gate, which are hot from the sun, then pull them back and open it myself. I get back in the car, drive through the gate, then get out, close it behind me, get back in the car, and drive slowly through the settlement. Before very long I arrive at what appears to be the old section; the place looks completely abandoned. To my right is a huge stable, and next to it a water tank on top of an old wooden tower, and to my left is a street, past which are several huts which look very similar to ones I saw in the film at the military museum in Yafa. This must be where the crime occurred. Maybe this hut is the one the platoon commander used as his quarters, and that older-looking one is where the girl was held and then raped by the rest of the soldiers. I get out of the car and approach the two huts. I stand in front of them for some time, contemplating them, then walk around them. After a while, I head toward a large storage building. But when I get closer, I realize that it's locked. Again I circle the huts, then the storage depot across the street, and suddenly fear descends on me. Or maybe it's been inside me this entire time and simply strikes whenever it wants, like now, for instance, so I hurry back to the car and try to calm myself. I have to calm down. I start the engine and drive back toward the settlement entrance. But instead of going through it, I turn left onto a side street a few meters before the entrance. I can't leave so easily, not after everything I've endured to get here. I keep driving, without heading anywhere in particular. On the left side of the street there are big new houses, expanses of pale green grass unfurling in front of them, while on the right there is a barbed-wire fence, and behind it sandy hills that rise silently to the sky. I keep driving around the settlement, which seems empty of any life, past closed door after closed door, until finally, behind an insect screen, I see a half-opened glass door. I stop the car in the middle of the street and jump out, shouting hello in English. But no one responds so I shout again, louder this time: Hello. After a moment, a young man who looks about eighteen years old peers out. I ask where the settlement's archives or museum are. He directs me to the main entrance and describes a little white building; that's where the museum and archive are, he tells me. I return to the car, where a feeling of fear submerges me again. But despite it, I keep driving until I reach the settlement's entrance. I pull over on the side of the road, stop the car, get out, and slam the door behind me, letting the sound merge with the birdsong that fills the air. I approach a little old white building which looks like the one the young man described. I knock on the door and wait in front of it for a while. No one answers. I call out hello in English, then call out again, louder. After a long pause, a reply comes from behind me. I turn toward the sound and find a man in his early seventies standing in front of me. I say hello for the third time, then ask if he knows whether there is anyone inside. He says the archive is closed, then asks what I want exactly. I tell him, stammering slightly, that I wanted to learn about the history of Nirim, and take a close look at a few documents, for some research I'm doing about the area, and that I've come a very long way specifically for this purpose. After a brief moment of silence, he replies that he is the person in charge of the museum and the archive, and that he'll open them just for me, even though officially they close at one p.m. I thank him enthusiastically, and as soon as he opens the door, my heart beats so loudly that it might scare off the birds. We go inside, sweat dripping from our faces. He introduces himself, gestures for me to sit at a big table in the middle of a nearly empty room, then approaches a white cabinet on the wall to the right of the front door. Quite hot, isn't it? he asks, opening little drawers in the cabinet, and taking out a few envelopes. Yes, unbearable, I reply, and he adds that he actually doesn't mind the heat. It reminds him of the weather in Australia, to a certain extent. He emigrated from Australia in the fifties, and has lived in Nirim since he arrived. And my name? I reply with the first non-Arab name that comes to mind. And my research? It's a study of the geography and social topography of the area, during the period between the late forties and early fifties. He returns to the table where I'm sitting, carrying several envelopes he's taken from the drawers, sits down near me, and begins removing dozens of photographs and spreading them over the table's extremely white surface. As he does, he explains that he's not a specialized researcher like I am. He's just fond of photography and history is all, that's why he founded this simple museum, in an attempt to preserve Nirim's history and archives. I ask him to tell me about the settlement's history as I start flipping through the photographs. And he begins speaking in a voice so calm and clear, so untouched by stuttering, stammering, or rambling, that it feels as if he is smoothly unraveling a delicate thread, one which cannot easily be cut. "Nirim's cornerstone was laid on the night of Yom Kippur in 1946. It was one of the eleven settlements established by members of Hashomer Hatzair and young Europeans who had arrived in the country at the end of the Second World War. They began constructing settlements in the Negev. At the time, the aim of their operation was to expand the territory of Jewish settlements in the south.

"And so, under the wing of darkness, and the protection and leadership of the Haganah, three hundred trucks carrying more than a thousand people departed for the Negev, without anyone opposing them or standing in their way, not even the British authorities, who did not know a thing about it, since arrangements for the operation were made in complete secrecy, without even the Jewish Agency's knowledge. An enthusiastic group of young men in twenty-five vehicles departed with that caravan and went as far south in the Negev as one could go, to a place near the city of Rafah and the border with Egypt. There, Nirim was founded in an area called Dangour, named after a wealthy Jewish Egyptian who had acquired some land in that part of the Negev in the late thirties.

"The high morale and youthful spirit of Nirim's founding group was particularly evident as they prepared for war. At the time, the likelihood of war breaking out was growing daily. During the day, they began digging trenches, carrying out military drills, setting up makeshift clinics and practicing giving first aid to the wounded, while at night they sang songs to accordion music and read excerpts from the Palmach booklet together. In general, the social and cultural atmosphere in Nirim was lively up until the eve of the war, even though its members soon became aware that the Egyptian Army was massing troops along the border, and that they could suffer a big attack, which is what eventually happened. After the establishment of the state of Israel was announced on May 14, 1948, Nirim was the first settlement to be attacked by the Egyptian Army. All the buildings were destroyed in the heavy shelling by artillery, eight of the founders were killed, and several others were wounded. But the rest of the members held their positions in the trenches, trying to ward off the attack with nothing more than rifles and machine guns. And although the Egyptian

Army was vastly superior in numbers and weapons, compared to the members of the settlement, it suffered heavy losses and was forced to retreat from its attack on Nirim, leaving the settlement behind as it advanced north.

"In the end, forty-nine members of Nirim, armed with only light weapons, held off a regular, fully equipped army numbering around a thousand. Many people attribute the miracle of Nirim's success to the members' determination: they kept communicating and moving between different fighting positions in the settlement, and eventually the Egyptian Army realized they were not going to surrender, so it decided to keep marching instead of losing more time.

"After the attack, as heavy shelling continued elsewhere, daily life in Nirim was conducted underground, in trenches and bunkers. The attack, and especially the deaths of eight young founders, some of whom had family members who had survived the Holocaust in Europe, left a deep mark on the character of Nirim. This is reflected in a phrase that members of the settlement had written on a piece of cloth and hung from a wall on the eve of the war during a May Day celebration. This phrase, and the wall on which it hung, remained unharmed after the attack, and are still celebrated here to this day."

At the end of his speech, he passes me a photograph of the lone wall standing amid the rubble, on which hangs a white banner, with a phrase in Hebrew that he translates for me: "Man, not the tank, shall prevail." Spread across the table are more photographs: a caravan of vehicles stranded in the sand, the area before the settlement was established, the founding members in gray shorts and short-sleeve shirts which look like uniforms, then different stages of the settlement as it was being constructed, including several huts and a big dining hall. There are also photographs of several members of the settlement sitting and speaking with a few Bedouin residents of the area, and another of them all looking at the camera and smiling. I ask about the relationship between Palestinian residents and Jewish immigrants during that period. Excellent, he replies; members of the settlement set up a tent for guests, to welcome Bedouins of the area, who often came to visit them and drink mint tea together. Before long, close friendships and deep trust developed between the two sides, and the Bedouins left their swords with the youth of Nirim. But these relationships ended when the war broke out. Why? Were there any confrontations or specific incidents during the war, or even afterward, that led to that? No, he says. But, he adds, such is war; sometimes it even severs ties between members of the same family. And after the war? Occasionally, he says, clashes did occur between members of the settlement and the few Arabs left in the area, whose livestock sometimes devoured crops on settlement land. Did that ever lead to someone being killed? A man or a woman, on either side? He replies that he doesn't know of any incidents like that. Then, after a moment of silence, he adds that the only incident he ever encountered was when he volunteered in a military unit formed after the end of the war, whose primary mission was to search for infiltrators in the area. What was the incident? I ask, trying to keep my heartbeats from choking my voice. He replies that one day, during a patrol, they found the body of a young Bedouin girl in a nearby well, and explains to me that when Arabs are suspicious about a girl's behavior, they kill her and throw her body in a well. Such a shame, he adds, that they have such customs.

After the War of Independence, he says, in conclusion, a decision was made to move the settlement here, about twenty-five kilometers north of the original location. Why? First, because this area is more secure, and second, because the average annual rainfall here is much higher than at the other location.

At the end of my visit, he offers me a booklet with lots of information about the settlement and its history. I thank him and head outside to where the car is parked, waiting patiently and loyally for me. And when I sit down behind the steering wheel and begin to flip through the booklet, I discover that most of the information I've just obtained is the same as what's included in its pages; the settlement even has a website, where anyone can find additional information. So this isn't the site of the crime, and not only that, but all the information I've gathered on this arduous trip I could have obtained while sitting in my house, at my table in front of the big window.

At least the booklet contains a small map of the settlement's previous location. According to what I've just discovered, and according to the booklet too, the place is called Dangour, not Nirim, named after the wider area prior to the settlement's construction. I start the engine and head toward the main entrance, where the guard is finally sitting at his post; he opens the gate for me, saving me the effort, and I set off, on a black road that leads me between silent yellow hills trembling nervously under the heft of a mirage. And even though it is still afternoon, I see no other cars on the roads I take, no living beings on the hills that extend on either side. Just a few trees, when occasionally I pass a grove of mango, avocado, or banana. And the further south I go, the stronger my impression that the area is completely deserted, until finally I arrive at my destination. It's on my left, and on my right is a military camp. They haven't left the area, then. I park the car on the side of the road, a little before the camp, and get out. The weather is still extremely hot, and the sun is strong. I walk on the asphalt, past dozens of pages ripped from porn magazines, which litter both sides of the road, and along the fence that encircles the camp. Behind it, I can see the tops of many tents, but no soldiers. I hesitate for a moment, reluctant to cross to the other side. Then, a few moments later, I cross the road and head straight for the site of the crime, without further delay. The place looks like a little park; the ground is sandy and uneven, and there are a few eucalyptus trees and wooden benches scattered around. On the far left stands a concrete structure, where written in Hebrew is the same phrase I saw in one of photographs at the Nirim museum: "Man, not the tank, shall prevail." I walk around the park, over the sand. The eucalyptus trees are now to my right, and directly in front of me is the concrete structure, so I head toward it, step inside and climb a staircase that leads me to the roof, where a vast scene unfolds before me, sandy plains, interspersed here and there with pale green fields, then groves of trees, then a wall, followed by rows of gray and white houses, dappled with the green of a few trees, which make the line of the horizon appear to meander confusedly. This is Rafah, which will soon swallow the sun as it sets. And to the right lie the sandy hills, and the expanses of mango, banana, and avocado groves, which I passed in the car a little while earlier. I turn and study the view to the left again; it's mostly obscured by the eucalyptus trees, which conceal any details of what lies beyond. Then, after some hesitation, I lift my gaze to the camp. I don't detect any movement inside. The tents are still, as are the military vehicles scattered around the camp. Cautiously, I turn my gaze toward the watchtowers, where the openings are too dark for me to know if there are soldiers inside observing me. Eventually, I leave the roof and descend the staircase, letting it lead me down through the layers of the structure, whose towering height isolates a person from their surroundings; inside, nothing but concrete can be seen in any direction. I'm on the verge of suffocating, so I quicken my steps until my feet touch the sand again. And there I wander around, searching for any remnant of trenches or huts. The only trace suggesting a past settlement or military camp is a small trench of sorts, in which the sandbags supporting the sides appear to be new and completely unworn. Then, on the sand, I notice human footprints. But they're not sharply imprinted; the outlines have faded. They could be from several days ago. Aside from these, nothing at all. There's nothing else to see on the sand, not even a small piece of garbage. Even the garbage bags hanging from metal rings on posts next to the wooden benches are empty, the plastic they're made from still clinging to itself. And although I find no details, neither major nor minor, to denounce the crime that occurred here twenty-five years to the day before I was born, I keep walking through the park. Later, as the sun nears the roofs of houses in Rafah, I walk across the grounds, then the road, get in the car, and leave.

I keep driving between the low, sandy hills, some of which are dotted with plants and some with trees, with no clear destination in mind but without straying far from the site. Eventually, I realize that I'm driving in circles, and that there's no use in roaming around like this, so I stop the car on the side of the road, get out, and walk into a grove of trees. On the sand lies a hose, neatly running from one tree to the next and coiled in equal-sized rings around each trunk. I walk between the rows of trees; the first ones are tall, and their leaves seem intensely green despite being covered by a thin layer of dust. Avocados hang from their branches. I reach toward one and press my finger to its rough skin, then I walk on toward a row of shorter trees behind this one. These are mango trees. My hand touches the smooth skin of their fruit, whose flesh is harder than that of the avocados. I walk on, past the banana plants behind them, until I reach the end of the grove and am welcomed by the last light of day pouring from between the huge leaves. I wander through them for a while, then suddenly I fall to the sand. I roll onto my back and stretch out, allowing my gaze to hang on the bleak pale-blue blue of the sky, while the faint light of the hour before sunset infiltrates between the banana leaves and flows over me. I lie there on the sand, allowing my feeling of helplessness to shift into feelings of deep loneliness. I am here in vain. I haven't found anything I've been searching for, and this journey hasn't added anything to what I knew about the incident when I started out. Loneliness gradually turns to anxiety, as the sunlight fades and night begins to fall. I have to get up and go back to the car. I push my body up to stand, and begin walking through the trees, which suddenly seem endless, no way out, so I start running as fast as I can until I reach the car, open the door, and collapse into the driver's seat. I have to leave the area immediately. I pick up the Israeli map from the passenger seat and study the route back to Ramallah. Road 232 to Road 34, turn left, keep going to Highway 40, turn right, take that until Road 443, and after that I remember the way. I return the map to the seat next to me, on top of the other maps, start the engine, and set off.

As soon as I get going in the car and leave the place behind, I calm down a little. Actually, maybe if I stay here longer I'll discover something, or find a thread that could lead me to new details about the incident, which could help me form some kind of picture of what the girl endured. As sunset approaches, I begin to think about spending the night here. Why not? The question is where, and it's a question I'll ask the first person I encounter. So I keep driving around for a while, on a network of intersecting straight narrow streets, where the asphalt forms black frames around stretches of yellow sand, until I arrive at a gas station shortly after sunset. First, I fill the tank, which is almost empty, seeing as I've been driving around all day. It's the first time in my life that I've done this myself, and being so clumsy, I spill some gasoline on my hands and pants. Then, with the smell of gasoline racing ahead of me, I head to the station attendant to pay. He's a nice young man, and naturally doesn't mind the smell of gasoline exuding from me, since he spends most of his time here at the station himself. I ask him if there is somewhere nearby I can spend the night, and he suggests I go to Nirim settlement; some people there rent out rooms to tourists such as myself. So Nirim again. According to the map, it isn't far from here, and the route is easy. And so I head straight to it. It's not long before I arrive at the barrier gate at the main entrance, and I don't see the guard at his station, so I get out of the car, push the gate open myself, get back in the car, drive through, get out, close the gate, then get back in and head toward the heart of the settlement. I drive past the huts where I initially thought the crime had been committed, and gaze at them indifferently this time. The feelings I'd had when I first saw them, of grief and then agitation, are now completely dispelled. I continue driving through the settlement, and only now do I notice that the streets are named after flowers. I've just turned onto Jasmine Street when I catch sight of a young man standing beside a car, next to another man whose upper half has disappeared into the trunk. I get out of the car, say hello, and ask if they know somewhere I might spend the night. The second man briefly emerges to see who is there, then his upper half vanishes again as he goes back to the contents of the trunk, while the young man replies that he usually rents out rooms like this himself, but unfortunately he doesn't have any vacant ones tonight. I ask, with some disappointment, if he knows of any other rooms he can direct me toward, and he suggests that I head back down this street and turn left before the end of the road, onto Narcissus Street. There's a guesthouse at the top of the street, on the left, and I might find a vacant room there. Then he adds, Just a minute, and he takes a mobile phone from a holster on his belt and calls someone. He's talking to the owner of the guesthouse on Narcissus Street, who in fact has one vacant room left: You're in luck. I thank him for his kindness before heading over there. It's starting to grow dark. When I arrive at the guesthouse on Narcissus Street, I find the owner waiting for me on the sidewalk. And even though he doesn't ask who I am, I introduce myself and tell him why I'm here, giving him the same reason I told the person in charge of Nirim's museum and archive, to avoid arousing any suspicion. The guesthouse owner leads me through a large garden, to a hut across from his house. Inside, the hut is clean and tidy. I pay in advance for the night, and outside I see that it's already here; as we walk back to the hut's entrance together, we're greeted by absolute darkness. The guesthouse owner leaves me and heads to his house, while I continue to the car, take my bag and the maps, lock the car, then go back to the hut, and as I'm setting my bag down on the kitchen table I notice the fridge, and realize that the last thing I've eaten is chewing gum. It's all I've had since this morning, so I head to the fridge and open it. There is a cake and two containers of yogurt inside. I eat some of the cake, though just a little, since I'm not sure if I'm allowed to or not. Perhaps the previous guests left it behind, so I eat a little more, then go outside. I turn off the light illuminating the hut's entrance and linger for a moment, until the hammock I'd noticed when I arrived materializes in the dark, hanging between two dwarf palms. I walk toward it through the velvety night and lie down, observing the gentle light of the distant stars scattered across the sky. I lie there for a long time without moving, so long that a light layer of dew begins to form on me. All of a sudden, I glimpse a dark black mass walking across the grass, heading toward me, and then it stops in front of the hammock. It's a dog. Immediately its presence drives fear into me. I repeatedly try to expel the dog, but it stands there motionless, while my fear intensifies, compelling me, in the end, to get off the hammock and return to the hut. Before I go inside, I look back at the dog. But there's no sign of it. It has vanished completely.

I enter the hut, and even though I'm exhausted and completely uninterested in washing, the smell of gasoline still clings to me, forcing me into the bathroom. I step into the shower, draw the curtain, then turn on the tap, and a stream of warm water rushes over my body with force so abundant and powerful that it reminds me I'm not in Ramallah, and I don't need to worry that if I don't quickly turn off the tap, I'll use up all the water in the tank and there won't be any left for the neighbors. I cover my skin with a thick layer of soap suds, trying to remove the smell of gasoline and the sweat and dust, which have collected on my body over the course of the day. Then I turn the tap back on and let the plentiful water flow over my body, washing away everything, even the memory of the bathroom in my house in Ramallah and its trickle of water. I have a hard time making myself turn off the tap and step out of the shower, until I'm nearly certain I've used more water during this shower than I usually do in a week of showering daily. With that realization, I quickly turn off the tap. Then I dry my body before wrapping it with a towel, and finally step out of the bathroom carrying my clothes, which still smell of gasoline and faintly of sweat. I walk over to the kitchen table, drape my shirt over the back of one chair and my pants over another to air them both out, hoping the smells will dissipate, then place my shoes under the table. On my way to bed, I pause at a small shelf with a slim collection of books, including travel guides to the region, cookbooks, and books about art. I pick up one of the art books and head to the bedroom. I get into bed, and the firm mattress is a sign that I'll soon be overtaken by a sense of comfort. I open the big heavy book I took with me. On one of the first pages is a painting of a man with a slightly reddish face, wearing a black suit and white shirt, sitting tranquilly on a chair. The book is about the expressionist art movement, which, as it goes on to say, was influenced by the killing and devastation that German artists experienced during the First World War. These experiences encouraged the transformation from classical styles of painting to radical distortions of the human figure and its surroundings. The lines that compose the many paintings in the book are indeed sharp, agitated, and distorted. I keep turning the pages until I come to excerpts of letters written by one of these artists to his wife. In a letter dated May 8, 1915, he wrote, "Yesterday we came across a cemetery that had been completely destroyed by shellfire. The graves had been blown up, and the coffins lay about in the most uncomfortable positions. The shells had unceremoniously exposed their distinguished occupants to the light of day, and bones, hair, and bits of clothing could be seen through cracks in the burst-open coffins." Another letter, dated May 21, 1915, says: "The trenches wound in meandering lines and white faces peered from dark dugouts—a lot of men were still preparing the positions, and everywhere among them there were graves. Where they sat, beside their dugouts, even between the sandbags, crosses stuck out. Corpses jammed in among them. It sounds like fiction—one man was frying po- tatoes on a grave next to his dugout. The existence of life here had already become a paradoxical joke." On another page, I see a painting of a naked girl lying on her stomach on the sand, as if she'd fallen onto it; her body is yellow, like the sand, and her short, tousled hair is black. I close the book and set it aside, then turn off the light and fall asleep, until I am awoken in the hours before dawn by the sound of a heavy explosion, followed a few moments later by another, then another, and another. I'm not dreaming. I listen intently to the sounds of the shelling, and the heaviness of the sound translates my distance from the place being bombed. It's far, past the Wall. In Gaza, or maybe Rafah. Bombing sounds very different depending on how close one is to the place being bombed, or how far. The rumblings from this shelling aren't strong at all, and the noise isn't unsettling; rather, it's a deep, heavy sound, like a languorous pounding on a massive drum. And the bombs causing it don't shake the building I'm in, even though the walls are thin and made of light wood; they don't shatter the glass, even though the windows are closed. And when I get out of bed and open the windows, the room isn't filled with a thick cloud of shuddersome dust; instead, what sneaks inside is the soft, tender air of dawn. I keep listening, my ears trained to the sound of repeated bombings, and I feel a strange closeness with Gaza, as well as a desire to hear the shelling from nearby, and to touch motes of dust from the buildings being bombed. The absence of dust brings an awareness of how profoundly far I am from anything familiar, and how impossible it will be to return. And so, before I'm completely consumed by anxiety and horror, I go back to bed and soon fall asleep.

In the early morning, I wake up and get dressed. The smell of sweat has slightly dissipated from my clothes, but not the smell of gasoline. I go to the car, get in, slam the door behind me, then start the engine and leave without seeing the owner of the guesthouse. I head for the site of the crime, because I don't know where else to go. The drive seems much shorter this time than it did yesterday, and I let myself be guided by the arched lines of the hills, then the groves of mango, avocado, and banana, as opposed to the maps. And when I arrive, I find the site as I left it yesterday, less hot maybe, since the day is still just beginning, and a thin layer of clouds has veiled the rays of the rising sun. I head to the concrete building, which greets me again with the words: "Man, not the tank, shall prevail," and I climb the staircase. From the roof, Rafah appears once more, bounding the horizon. Smoke from last night's shelling rises silently from the city before dissipating into the morning's pale blue sky, its color nearly indistinguishable from the gray wall that conceals most of the city's houses behind it. A few colleagues at my new job, who are very nice, come from Rafah and other parts of Gaza. So I let my eyes absorb the scene that appears before me for these colleagues, who have been waiting many years for permits that would allow them to visit.

I descend the staircase, then head to a sandy hill nearby and sit down under the shade of a eucalyptus tree. I open my bag and take out a container of yogurt that I took from the fridge in the hut in the settlement, and a little spoon I took too, and start eating. The yogurt is so white that every once in a while the glare hurts my eyes as they slowly wander over the area, moving among the same details I observed yesterday. Trees sinking their trunks into the sand, the small reconstructed trench, the phrase inscribed on the concrete building, the military camp on the other side of the road. When I finish eating the yogurt, I push myself up, pressing my palms into the ground to stand, and notice what appear to be fresh dog-paw-shaped prints in the sand next to where I'd been sitting. Then I realize that there are tracks all around. With this discovery, the fear inside me awakens again. I walk toward the car, trying to stay calm in case soldiers in the camp watchtowers are observing me. And so I walk as slowly as I can, letting my gaze wander from the trunks of the trees to their desiccated leaves, to the wooden park benches. Then to the sand around the trench, compressed from being walked on so frequently. My legs want me to rush to the car and leave this place immediately, but then I remember the chewing gum. I reach into my bag, take out a pack of gum, empty two pieces into my mouth, then put the pack in my pants pocket. I start chewing, and with my left hand I raise the empty yogurt container I'm carrying up to my eyes, focusing on reading what's written there until I reach the car. I open the door, put my bag on the passenger seat next to me, and the empty yogurt container behind the emergency brake, then calmly start the engine and begin driving along the fence surrounding the military camp, which I try to avoid looking at as much as possible; instead I examine the area around the park. I don't turn back the way I came, but drive in the opposite direction, and after a few meters the road comes to a T. Several tanks and military vehicles line the road to the right, which leads toward Rafah; dozens of soldiers stand around them, some swaying left and right as they shift their weight and exchange brief conversations with each other. It looks like they're about to launch a ground invasion on Rafah. I turn left, on a road that sends me far from all of Gaza and the things that will befall it. I continue heading east, circling aimlessly like an agitated fly, driving around sandy hills and expanses, and past rows of cypress or eucalyptus trees that occasionally cut through them. Time keeps passing, without me reaching a decision on what I ought to do. Eventually, I stop the car on the roadside, pick up the maps from the seat next to me, and open the Israeli one, searching for the number of the road I'm on. Here, this is as far as I've gone. My eyes follow the road as it leads east, and to the north I notice several towns and villages with Arabic names, all of which are concentrated in an area shaped like a triangle, framed by three intersecting roads. Outside this triangle, most of the southern Naqab appears to be uninhabited, with the exception of a few points designated as military training zones, settlements, or private Israeli farms. I examine the triangle area again, and the names of towns which I'm reading for the first time. After a while, I put the map back on the passenger seat, take the chewing gum from my mouth and deposit it in the ashtray, and start heading north. I gradually begin seeing more cars on the road, which makes the area appear less deserted. More rocks and stones cast their sharp shadows across the plateaus, where the ground has turned from pale yellow sand to white dust. I keep driving until I notice a dirt road branching off on the left, which looks wide enough for a car, so I quickly flip my left indicator, slow down, and turn onto it. The gravel that covers the road makes it easy to drive on, but despite how cautiously I'm driving, thick clouds of dust rise up and swiftly form a halo that obscures the scene behind me. In front of me, the view is dominated by desolate, barren hills, which are rendered harsher by the late morning sun and many scattered stones. After some minutes, the tops of a few huts appear, then disappear behind the hills, then reappear again and again as I continue down the road. Only when I'm a few meters away do they come into full view. And there, a dog leaps up to meet me and races toward the car, barking fiercely; I do my best to avoid it and not run it over, but it doesn't seem to notice and keeps chasing the car. When I come to a stop it keeps barking and runs in circles in front of the car, forcing me to stay inside, and so I wait for it to calm down and leave, or for someone to emerge from one of the huts and rescue me. But nothing of the sort happens. I look around the area, searching for anyone as I examine the huts, some of which are constructed entirely of corrugated zinc panels, while others have brick walls and roofs made of zinc panels covered with plastic sheeting and finally rocks, probably put there to keep the sheeting in place in the wind. Aside from the huts, there are a few pens with no livestock inside, their gates hanging open. The place seems practically deserted. No one has come out to greet me, no one has peered out to investigate the constant barking, or even the rumbling car and dust clouds that preceded it. I pick up the Israeli map again, searching for an indication of this little village, but I find no trace. Blank yellow space occupies the area on the map where I imagine its location to be. I fold the map and return it to the seat beside me. Perhaps this is one of the unrecognized villages in the Naqab that one hears about. I look at the water tanks, then the several old vehicles scattered around; some have missing tires and are propped up by bricks, and most of their doors, steering wheels, lights, and seats are missing too. I don't know how long I can remain in the car, where the heat is becoming unbearable. The dog is still besieging me, although its barking has calmed a little. But as soon as I start opening the window to let in some air, it starts barking frantically again, so I quickly roll up the window, leaving it open just a crack, then continue inspecting my surroundings. I've counted six huts when I suddenly glimpse what looks like the silhouette of somebody's head, maybe a girl's, peering out from the entrance to one of the huts, but it vanishes just as quickly, while I'm still trying to open the window, to stick out my head and shout hello. At this, the dog leaps up and starts barking fiercely again, so I quickly roll up the window and try to send my voice through the narrow opening instead, calling out several times toward the dim doorway into which the shadow disappeared. But she doesn't respond;

all I hear is the barking, which drowns out my voice. Eventually I surrender to silence, giving up hope of anyone responding, and gradually I begin to wonder whether I'd really seen the girl, or if I'd only imagined her. The dog's barking gradually quietens too, but it doesn't abandon the car. Instead, it lies down in front of it, on the pale sandy ground. When I notice this, I lean very carefully toward the passenger side, trying as hard as I can not to attract the dog's attention, and slowly open the window, hoping to let in some air and ease the heat that is intensifying inside the car, but nothing of the sort happens, and instead extreme heat assails me from every side. And as the silence continues, I sink into my seat, trying to decide what to do. I really don't know. After a few moments, I shift in my seat, then look back at the dog, and find him looking at me. I turn my gaze toward the entrance of the hut where I glimpsed the girl's shadow a little while ago; still only darkness peers out. I must have imagined the girl. I stare at the entrances and the closed windows of the other huts, hoping to see someone appear, and then turn my gaze to a water tank nearby, where a blue barrel nearly full of water is sitting directly under the tap. The place isn't entirely deserted. I look at the livestock pens, at the zinc panels and scrap metal they're constructed from, then at the old vehicles sitting around the area. Even though everything is man-made, when taken together it seems to be in perfect harmony with nature. Finally, I reach for the keys, start the engine, and turn the car around, heading back the way I came. The dog shoots up on all fours, starts barking again, and begins to follow me. I can see it in the rearview mirror, running behind me, until clouds of dust rise into the air, concealing the dog, and the huts and hills, completely from my sight. I reach the main road and turn right toward the southwestern part of the Naqab, without a clear reason, as if I'm no longer able to leave the area. I keep driving, past barren hills that slowly turn into pale yellow sand again, while the traffic diminishes until there are no other cars. Now, the only movement belongs to the mirage, which makes the roads and hills waver nervously. Shadows begin to appear, but they vanish the moment I look at them, until suddenly I catch sight of an old woman standing on the side of the road before an intersection. I stop the car alongside her. I roll down the window and ask if I can help her with something, or if she'd like me to take her somewhere.

The old woman gets into the car. She settles into the passenger seat beside me and we set off, both taking refuge in the silence, and each of our gazes hanging on different parts of the scene surrounding us. I'm looking forward, at the road which cuts through the rippling hills, where the color of earth has changed from pale yellow to light brown, and she looks out to the right; I can tell by the angle of her head, which is covered with a scarf, black like her black dress. I steal glances at her as I drive, at part of her face, which is lined with sharp wrinkles, then at her hands, which she lets rest in her lap, on the fabric of her black dress, and they seem stronger than any hands I've seen in my life. They're traced with blue veins that recall the lines on the maps I tossed into the back seat when I stopped the car to take her with me. She's probably in her seventies. The girl would have been around the same age now, most likely, if she hadn't been killed. Maybe this old woman has heard about the incident, since incidents like that would have reached the ears of everyone living in the Naqab, terrorizing them all, and no one who heard about it would be able to forget. I could start by asking her about the area, and how long she's lived here, then gradually transition to asking about the incident, and if she knows anything about it. But the words do not emerge from my mouth. The silence between us stretches on, as vast as nature's silence expanding around us, and tightens its grip, until the old woman suddenly asks me to stop, and so I do, and she gets out. But before she does, she looks directly into my eyes. Then she turns and quietly retreats toward a sandy path to the left, which no one traveling on the asphalt road would notice or imagine might lead somewhere. The old woman continues to walk on the path until every trace of her vanishes into the sandy hills, while I set off in the car, accompanied by the feeling of her absence in the seat beside me, and then by regret, because I could not bring myself to ask her about the incident. How clumsy! It was she, not the military museums or the settlements and their archives, who might hold a detail that could help me uncover the incident as experienced by the girl. And finally arrive at the whole truth. The greater the distance between us grows, the greater too my realization, and my regret. Suddenly I stop the car, turn around and head back the way I came, until I reach the place where the old woman got out. I park the car on the side of the road and start searching through all the maps I possess for a town or village on the left, where the old woman might have gone. But there's no sign of any cluster of houses. The Israeli map just shows scattered dots far from the road, indicating a military training zone and a shooting range. I get out of the car and cross the road toward the narrow sandy path I saw her take. I follow it for several paces, hoping I might discover something behind the dunes it leads me toward, but all that follows these dunes are more dunes. I consider driving the car down this path. I could do it, if I drive carefully. So I retrace my steps back to the main road, get in the car, and head toward the path. It leads me between sandy hills, which soon reveal a view unlike everything I've seen until this point. As the car makes its way between the yellow hills, thorn acacia, terebinth trees, and cane grass suddenly appear, nestled in the heart of the hills.

There must be a spring here. I don't resist the urge to head in its direction, despite a sign indicating that this is a military zone, something one often encounters in Area B. When I've nearly reached the trees, I stop the car, get out, and begin walking toward them. A blazing silence reigns, and the sound of my steps on the sand stirs a feeling of apprehension inside me, so I try to tread carefully, making my footfall as light as I can, hardly noticing anything other than the patches of earth where my feet land. I keep walking like this until I notice something lying on the sand. I get a little closer, then lean over, bringing my eyes close to it. It's a bullet casing. I reach out my hand and pick it up. I lift the casing in front of my face to inspect it, and when I do, I notice that a few meters away, among the thorn acacia trees, is a group of camels, standing perfectly still and staring at me, and I remain perfectly still too. I don't know what these camels are doing here in a firing range. Two camels on the right turn away from me and begin moving toward the nearby trees, hopping nimbly over what seems like a crack in the sand and disappearing behind the vegetation. Then the four remaining camels follow the first two, walking steadily across the sand, which muffles the sound of their steps, and vanish behind the same trees. I stand up, the bullet casing still in my right hand, and turn back toward the car, leaving the camels to graze in peace. And when I do, I see a group of soldiers in the middle of this vast scene, standing in silence, looking in my direction. Instantly a wave of heat sweeps over me, and my body starts to sweat. I have to calm down, immediately. Being tense won't change the course of things. Then there's the bullet casing in my hand; I open my fingers and it falls softly to the sand. I have to keep walking, calmly and steadily, without paying attention to them, back to the car. But one of the soldiers shouts in my direction, ordering me to stop where I am, and the others raise their guns at me. Immediately the sound of my pulse starts beating violently in my head, and numbness extends through my entire body, paralyzing it. They must have noticed the little white car which entered the military zone, and which would have definitely aroused suspicion; maybe they contacted the police, who have the right to obtain whatever information they want, including the identity of the owner of this little white car, and they discovered it belongs to a Palestinian car rental company, based in Area A, and is rented by a man who is also a resident of Area A, not by a woman like the one they're aiming their weapons at, right at this moment. I have to calm down. I must be overreacting. Yes, just like usual. My chewing gum. Where is it? I have to calm down. I reach my hand toward my pocket, for the pack of chewing gum.

And suddenly, something like a sharp flame pierces my hand, then my chest, followed by the distant sound of gunshots.

New Directions Paperbooks — a partial listing

Clarice Lispector, The Hour of the Star
  The Passion According to G. H.
Federico García Lorca, Selected Poems*
  Three Tragedies
Nathaniel Mackey, Splay Anthem
Xavier de Maistre, Voyage Around My Room
Stéphane Mallarmé, Selected Poetry and Prose*
Javier Marías, Your Face Tomorrow (3 volumes)
Bernadette Mayer, The Bernadete Mayer Reader
  Midwinter Day
Carson McCullers, The Member of the Wedding
Thomas Merton, New Seeds of Contemplation
  The Way of Chuang Tzu
Henri Michaux, A Barbarian in Asia
Dunya Mikhail, The Beekeeper
Henry Miller, The Colossus of Maroussi
  Big Sur & the Oranges of Hieronymus Bosch
Yukio Mishima, Confessions of a Mask
  Death in Midsummer
  Star
Eugenio Montale, Selected Poems*
Vladimir Nabokov, Laughter in the Dark
  Nikolai Gogol
  The Real Life of Sebastian Knight
Raduan Nassar, A Cup of Rage
Pablo Neruda, The Captain's Verses*
  Love Poems*
Charles Olson, Selected Writings
Mary Oppen, Meaning a Life
George Oppen, New Collected Poems
Wilfred Owen, Collected Poems
Hiroko Oyamada, The Factory
Michael Palmer, The Laughter of the Sphinx
Nicanor Parra, Antipoems*
Boris Pasternak, Safe Conduct
Kenneth Patchen
  Memoirs of a Shy Pornographer
Octavio Paz, Poems of Octavio Paz
Victor Pelevin, Omon Ra
Alejandra Pizarnik
  Extracting the Stone of Madness
Ezra Pound, The Cantos
  New Selected Poems and Translations
Raymond Queneau, Exercises in Style
Qian Zhongshu, Fortress Besieged
Raja Rao, Kanthapura
Herbert Read, The Green Child
Kenneth Rexroth, Selected Poems
Keith Ridgway, Hawthorn & Child

Rainer Maria Rilke
  Poems from the Book of Hours
Arthur Rimbaud, Illuminations*
  A Season in Hell and The Drunken Boat*
Evelio Rosero, The Armies
Fran Ross, Oreo
Joseph Roth, The Emperor's Tomb
  The Hotel Years
Raymond Roussel, Locus Solus
Ihara Saikaku, The Life of an Amorous Woman
Nathalie Sarraute, Tropisms
Jean-Paul Sartre, Nausea
Delmore Schwartz
  In Dreams Begin Responsibilities
Hasan Shah, The Dancing Girl
W. G. Sebald, The Emigrants
  The Rings of Saturn
Anne Serre, The Governesses
Stevie Smith, Best Poems
Gary Snyder, Turtle Island
Muriel Spark, The Driver's Seat
  The Girls of Slender Means
  Loitering with Intent
Antonio Tabucchi, Pereira Maintains
Junichiro Tanizaki, The Maids
Yoko Tawada, The Emissary
  Memoirs of a Polar Bear
Dylan Thomas, A Child's Christmas in Wales
  Collected Poems
Uwe Timm, The Invention of Curried Sausage
Tomas Tranströmer, The Great Enigma
Leonid Tsypkin, Summer in Baden-Baden
Tu Fu, Selected Poems
Paul Valéry, Selected Writings
Enrique Vila-Matas, Bartleby & Co.
Elio Vittorini, Conversations in Sicily
Rosmarie Waldrop, Gap Gardening
Robert Walser, The Assistant
  The Tanners
  The Walk
Eliot Weinberger, An Elemental Thing
  The Ghosts of Birds
Nathanael West, The Day of the Locust
  Miss Lonelyhearts
Tennessee Williams, The Glass Menagerie
  A Streetcar Named Desire
William Carlos Williams, Selected Poems
  Spring and All
Louis Zukofsky, "A"

*BILINGUAL EDITION

For a complete listing, request a free catalog from New Directions, 80 8th Avenue, New York, NY 10011
or visit us online at ndbooks.com